Adventures of a Bitterroot Boy

George Reeves

Thanks to Tig for putting up with me while I wrote these stories. The proofreaders including Dan, Lis, Jayne, Carol and Jeff helped me greatly. Your perusal of this preposterous publication is immensely appreciated. Please pardon my cadence commitment and contempt of commas.

Stories:

The Self Made Family
Giant Montana Pelicans
Ravalli County Rebels
Montana Misfits
The Cub Scout Caper
Swimming Hole Submarine
The Bitterroot Brigade

The Self Made Family

Butch Reynolds volunteered for the U.S. Army when he was seventeen. Four years later the 101st Airborne paratrooper's hitch finished. The "Screaming Eagle" received an honorable discharge in 1965. Butch's enlistment ended two weeks before his unit shipped out to Vietnam.

The former master parachute rigger returned to Montana on a Missoula bound Greyhound bus with his wife Mary and an infant son named Gavin. Butch's brother Steve picked the travelers up. The leadfoot then dropped them off at Joe and Kate Reynold's home. Their property was located near Hamilton.

Grandma Kate overtly disdained her stepson and his wife. Grandpa Joe's second spouse was determined to expel the intruders. It only took twelve hours. She evicted the interlopers after an acrimonious breakfast table altercation with Mary. Butch's Aunt Ruby gave the outcasts refuge until they found housing.

Dunbar's Sawmill hired Butch and he rented a three room cabin in Woodside. The crossroads community consisted of five tiny houses with an untidy small store that sold overpriced groceries. Butch's wages were low at the lumberyard and he didn't own a car. When winter came the striver hiked on Highway 93's snow packed surface.

Butch was an idealist. He desired a different way of life than his colleagues. If the millworkers supported their families they remained satisfied. The sawyers didn't expect more. Unlike Butch the woodcutters rejected risks.

The turtles had an insubordinate hare amongst them. Butch's observations irritated coworkers who listened unhappily when he explained, "Guys who make big bucks don't bust their humps." The misfit quit his job after a year and became an automobile salesman.

Mary's adjustment to the Treasure State was difficult. She had grown up as a high society Nashville girl. Her father Arthur operated an eminent Cadillac dealership. His clientele included Chet Atkins and Waylon Jennings. Mary's mother Grace ran a spotless six bedroom abode with authority. The Cornwell's had an expansive four car garage, horse stables and employed servants. Despite her privileged upbringing Mary traded the safety of Tennessee for a chancy destiny in Montana.

An amiable Ravalli County neighbor introduced herself to Mary. When Connie delivered welcome cookies she confided, "I went without a car during the first two years of my marriage." The considerate ally provided rides to grocery stores. Connie shared information about bargains for domestic necessities and food. The acquaintances drank coffee while their children cavorted. An affable friendship formed.

As time elapsed Mary adapted. The once spoiled socialite became a resilient rural lady. She got tougher. The transplant upped family revenue. Mary pitched in at the canning factory with Connie and sold Tupperware to make ends meet. Throughout the turbulent period Mary's steadfastness persisted. The stand by your man wife relished her adventurous existence. Mary was glad she hadn't wed an elitist from Belle Meade, Tennessee.

When Butch was twenty four Mary gave birth. The loving parents cherished a girl named Sara. Gavin responded conversely. He abhorred the attention usurper. The perturbed boy vehemently voiced, "I wish some stupid stork would take that cranky cabbage patch baby away." Gavin petulantly presumed his sister had an irreversible family position after the Reynolds leased a three bedroom house in Hamilton.

Butch's paychecks provided income periodically. Most of the dreamer's positions lasted less than six months. He ascertained requisite lessons along the way. Folks found Butch's aspirations far-fetched. Skeptics didn't deduce that their doubts and denunciations were his catalysts. Their criticism motivated him. He read sales technique books to educate himself. The ambitious learner also acquired management and marketing knowledge.

Twenty six year old Montanans seldomly started an autonomous business. Most men held the same trade as their fathers. Butch idled at his Bell-McCall Company desk when he dredged up a lucrative opportunity. The salesman perused an in depth *Popular Mechanics* magazine article about a manufacturing concept. Butch became convinced he should build an ingenious and profitable product that wasn't widely available. The solution seeker inferred he would be a trailblazer.

Butch initiated an improvised get rich quest. The proactive planner outpaced potential competition. He intuited the endeavor needed to be confidential. No one knew the undertaking's components or its sequestered procedures. The independent thinker worked alone and kept both garage doors padlocked when he was gone. Even Mary didn't have a key.

The forecaster forged ahead. Butch spent several more evenings on his project. The obsessive effort didn't go unnoticed by Mary. She continuously complained, "Why won't you tell me?" Butch eluded explanations when he related, "You'll find out soon enough."

Stealthy deeds in Butch's exclusive workshop progressed. Gavin remained restless while he heard the sounds of saws, drills and hammers until 9pm. Butch puttered past midnight but he was quiet. Hamilton denizens liked tranquility and well enforced noise ordinances.

Gavin came of age amidst an ethical environment. Words and actions caused consequences. People lived by the Golden Rule. Six year old Gavin obeyed the Bitterroot Valley's unwritten code decorously. The youngster discerned neighborliness and how a polite populace dealt with bad apples. An individual had two options; behave respectfully or leave. Many nuisances were banished to Billings and beyond.

Those who trespassed against this ethos met rapid retribution. The previous July a motorcycle pack guzzled liquor while they raced choppers on Hamilton's Main Street. Approximately thirty miscreants called the Bandoleros menaced for almost an hour. The California club provoked a Montana vigilante justice showdown. An outraged militia armed with shotguns, rifles, pistols, ax handles, tire irons, baseball bats and sheep shears hunted the rowdy roughnecks down. The vengeful posse shaved assorted long haired heads. Pickup trucks and hot rods chased the bloodied gang across Lost Trail Pass. The degenerates never revisited Ravalli County.

Butch's covert comportment sustained and Mary's antagonism escalated. When he stepped towards the backdoor during his cryptic crusade's fifth week she chastised, "For heaven's sake what's going on out there?" Butch grimaced and huffed. He tersely replied, "I'll tell you in a couple of days." Mary was rankled by her husband's sneakiness so she remonstrated, "I married an insane mad scientist. You're like Dr. Frankenstein. It's not normal."

The nonconformist revealed his clandestine creation six weeks after he began. Gavin waited in the garage's double car entryway anxiously. The exuberant child couldn't stand still. He did a perky pee pee prance. An intricately feathered headdress and ankle bells would've befitted him. Gavin hopped foot to foot like a Pow Wow dancer. Inertia wasn't the vivacious boy's forte.

Mary stood beside her son. She acted aloofly apathetic. The impatient mother held Sara's hand and chewed spearmint gum agitatedly. Gavin's Uncle Steve paced in the alley while he smoked an unfiltered Lucky Strike. Butch crushed a Pall Mall butt into an ashtray, turned and faced a tarp covered object. His brainchild sat atop six sawhorses.

Butch mimicked an oratorical carnival barker when he clutched the canvas's corner and shouted, "I proudly present a revolutionary RV industry revelation." The pitchman performed prestigiously. Butch snatched the veil away like an extraordinary Vaudeville skit tablecloth.

A miniature camper with strange dimensions appeared. The mystery likened to an enigmatic disc sighted in Roswell, New Mexico. It was unidentifiable. Nobody recognized the peculiarity. Butch broke the ice when he inquired, "What do you guys think?"

Many theories ran through the onlookers' minds as reticence carried on. Was the contrivance a magic prop that umpteen circus clowns disappeared into? Maybe the arcane item exemplified an imported European caravan. The French and Italians did drive dinky vehicles afterall. Asia also had a myriad of microphilia meccas. The four bewildered bystanders couldn't classify Butch's construction. Mary stopped the silence when she carped, "Is it an Oompa Loompa apartment?"

Butch resented Mary's malicious mockery. Frustration flooded the futurist. He walked to the workbench and lit a cigarette. Tension hung thickly in an uncomfortable atmosphere. Gavin hurriedly glanced westward to avert the mean spirited moment. He gazed at Downing Mountain and sympathized.

Gavin glimpsed towards the garage. Butch had regained composure. The concerned son was relieved his father's aggravation subsided. Steve soothed the situation succinctly. The comrade contested, "Whatever that thingamabob is it's cool."

Butch calmed down enough to proceed. He exasperatedly apprised, "It's a pickup topper. Some people call them pickup canopies. They sit on trucks like campers. Pickup toppers keep stuff safe and dry. I read an article that indicated pickup canopies are in high demand so I ordered the plans. I haven't seen any pickup bed covers locally."

Gavin stood slack jawed while he contemplated his father's triumph. After a lapse the imp vigorously jumped vertically. Gavin sprang like an ecstatic kangaroo. He spun and stomped the garage's dirt floor. Dust swirled at the blithe boy's feet. Gavin twirled a two step as he marveled, "The topper's terrific!"

Mary didn't share her son's adulation. The negative nitpicker grabbed both children's hands and bustled away. She shrilly sneered, "How much money did you spend on an impractical six week snipe hunt?" Butch eyed his brother and tacitly dared him to say anything. Steve was soundless. He stayed silent until Butch shrugged and apologized, "Sorry I shouldn't have dragged you into this mess."

The prototype canopy was scaled for compact pickup trucks. A smaller version enabled Butch to affordably rectify glitches. The topper's measurements fit his Ford Courier. Butch postulated if no one bought the pickup bed cover he could use it himself. The forerunner had faith that wouldn't be necessary.

Butch's pickup topper was unique. The trendsetter followed specifications with one deviation. Butch improved the configuration when he added an innovative front window. It opened between the pickup cab and canopy interior. The sturdy truck bed cover had two sliding side windows. A clear plexiglass rear access door lifted away from the tailgate.

Gavin stared out of an open bedroom window as his father and uncle installed the canopy. It adjoined perfectly. Steve inspected the flawless fabrication as he praised, "That's classy."

Butch clamped the pickup bed cover down and retrieved three signs a neighbor painted. The red cardboard with black print placards denoted, "Pickup Topper for Sale. $300.00." He taped the advertisements inside his canopy's windows and directed, "Let's get outta here." Butch resolved to rouse rubberneckers so he cruised around town extensively. The promoter then selected an efficient display location. Butch set up shop in the Safeway store parking lot.

Five minutes later a mud stained and dented Ford Courier pickup pulled up beside Butch's exhibit. An Australian shepherd sat in the vehicle's passenger seat. A rotund rancher climbed out and approached the Reynolds brothers. They stood in front of the pickup topper nonchalantly. The middle aged man drawled, "Howdy. Rory McKay's the name. Angus beef is my game." He pointed at his diminutive truck and averred, "It's a lot cheaper to drive an imported go kart. I only use the American made F250 when I need to."

Rory was a hardened haggler. The cunning cattleman negotiated with an effective method he used habitually. Rory scanned the topper, shook his head sideways and feigned disinterest. He then applied another reliable tactic. Rory diminished the canopy's significance fervently. The seasoned storyteller pretended to have Butch's welfare at heart as he proposed, "Perhaps I could help you partner. There aren't too many of these gizmos around. I guess nobody wants one. $200.00 seems fair."

Butch perceived the bovine breeder's ploy proficiently. The purposeful peddler was prepared for Rory's plot. He put a poker face on. Butch intoned friendliness when he appropriately avowed, "You're correct Sir. There's nothing like this pickup topper in the Bitterroot Valley. Where else are you going to find an immaculate new custom pickup canopy that fits on your truck? I've gotta have $300.00."

Rory cringed like he had been punched in the gut inhumanly. The wily wrangler was familiar with financial figure feuds so he continued his charade. Rory coughed and convulsed as though the pickup canopy's cost choked him. The appalled drover moaned, "$300.00 is awfully steep. How's about $250.00?"

Butch remained placid and paused. He assimilated superior sales strategy. Emotional engagement of prospects produced results. Hasty decisions were germinated when individuals fretted. If buyers worried a commodity could be taken away they craved it more.

Rory nervously shuffled his rattlesnake skin boots. Butch outmaneuvered the stockman psychologically as he stipulated, "My neighbor wants this topper. Maybe I'll make him an identical one. If you've got $275.00 you can take her home today." Rory's twitches rivaled a wiggly cutthroat trout hooked on an elk hair caddis fly. The cowpoke shook hands with Butch and exclaimed, "You betcha."

Rory removed wadded cash from his pocket. The big bellied buckaroo boorishly boasted, "I'm a deadly dickerer. This contraption will be handy." Rory counted $275.00 and surrendered the bills as he suggested, "Would you fellers load the doohickey on my Japanese jalopy while I shop?" Butch crammed the wrinkled currency in his pants pocket. The payee promised, "Sure. We'll attach it right now."

Steve and Butch fastened the canopy onto Rory's truck. They met the prideful pickup topper owner as he exited an automated Safeway store swinging door. Butch gave his customer five freshly printed business cards. The systematized string puller mentioned, "I'd be grateful if you tell your friends." Steve rounded up a Pabst Blue Ribbon six pack from the cooler while Butch and Rory conversed.

Both brothers thwarted Mary's hawk-like vision when they surreptitiously arrived from the alley's far side. The cohorts then sat on lawn chairs. Butch savored an unprecedented victory as he and his sibling sipped their brews. Steve earnestly extolled, "Butch you could sell snow cones to Eskimos."

Gavin saw Butch through his bedroom window. The keen kid abandoned a Hot Wheels crash and dashed downstairs while he yelled, "Dad came back!" Mary watched her son sprint outside. She put Sara on her hip and scurried to her husband swiftly. The pessimist protested, "What are you two Rockefellers up to?" Butch uttered an instant reply. He boldly recommended, "Hey Gavin. Take a look in the garage."

Butch's enthusiastic son ran inside the building and viewed his father's truck. Gavin then bolted to the yard before he blurted, "Where did the topper go?" Butch smiled with an ivory toothed grin the Cheshire Cat would've envied and waved a cash filled money clip at Mary. The showoff spouted, "Sold it for $275.00." Gavin leapt like an intoxicated leprechaun. The whippersnapper whooped, "Awesome!" Sara cuddled her Raggedy Ann doll and giggled.

Mary rarely lauded Butch's achievements. The pugnacious pragmatist atypically complimented, "Good job Honey." Gavin's frenzied Irish jig intensified. The ebullient scamp appended accolades as he hollered, "Hooray!" Steve celebrated cheerfully. He reported the gainful parley with Rory vividly. The admirer announced, "You should've seen him. Butch could've chatted that cornball out of his cowboy boots. He was slicker than a whistle."

The earnings were an encouraging blessing. Butch already had a trademarked company name and ninety five business cards. The pickup bed cap pioneer pressured Mary to reinvest. She agreed with her husband's agenda if he retained his current vocation.

Butch enumerated an initial pickup topper expense list. The numbers wizard calculated $150.00 profit. Butch prudently used the $275.00 dollars he received from Rory to assemble two pickup canopies. The busy builder had orders for both pickup toppers within a week. Butch streamlined manufacturing and strove zealously. The Montana maverick recurrently labored all night. He quit car sales after four months of tenacious toil.

The emergent establishment expanded exponentially. Butch financed an industrial zoned lot and erected a ten thousand square foot factory. His firm employed seven craftsmen. An office sat on the company's property. A life sized fiberglass mountain lion stood in front of the structure. Stainless steel letters attached to the statue's granite boulder base read "Cougar Manufacturing Incorporated." Other enhancements were implemented. Butch upgraded his transportation with an umber colored low mileage used Ford Ltd two-door hardtop. A Mack truck and canopy hauler trailer augmented infrastructure.

Mary became Butch's most crucial backer. She increasingly spent time at Cougar Manufacturing Incorporated's headquarters while her husband was elsewhere. Butch worked long hours. He split his schedule between logistics and sales. The engrossed executive excelled. His micro enterprise developed into an actual corporation.

Conditions trended upward for Gavin. The go-getter emulated his parent's fortitude. Gavin supplemented a chore allowance when he mowed neighbor's yards and shoveled snow. The eager beaver also went door to door as an assiduous W. Atlee Burpee & Co. representative. Gavin opened a passbook savings account at the Ravalli County Bank and replenished an enameled metal coin safe. The money maker amassed a modicum of material possessions. Gavin's acquisitions included an Eagle Claw tackle box that contained multiple Mepps spinning lures.

The industrious youth's friends Mike and Danny detected a difference in his circumstances. One afternoon the pals went to Gavin's kitchen for an appetizing snack. Mary apportioned refreshments and Mike commended, "Gavin you must be wealthy. Your mom gave us two Ding Dongs and Coca-Cola." Danny was also astonished. The boisterous boy gulped a Hostess treat bite and queried, "Mrs. Reynolds is it true what my father says about Mr. Reynolds? He calls him an entremanure." Danny's unintentional quip amused Mary. She folded a dish towel and drolly asserted, "Yes dear. My husband's more of an entremanure than you'll ever know."

Butch's road trips lasted for weeks. He communicated with most RV retailers in four states. Clients demanded perks. The effectual vendor performed pitches at burlesque lounges or seedy bars. Proprietors were provided a "good time" and salacious rendezvouses secured sales. When Butch reappeared from his travels he usually slept an entire day.

Occasionally Butch's escapades caused issues. One morning he was absent and Mary waited to ambush him. She stood by the kitchen counter bitterly. The enraged wife blended banana bread batter. Gavin sat at the table and Sara occupied a high chair. The edgy children ate egg salad sandwiches noiselessly.

It was around noon when Butch parked his car and crept through the backdoor furtively. The hungover husband frowned while Mary barked, "Where the heck have you been? You look like an exhausted wet Labrador retriever after duck hunting."

Butch rubbed a bloodshot eye. He promptly professed, "I had an evening appointment and the roads were icy. What's gotten into you?" A wrath that would've frightened Linda Blair possessed Mary as she shrieked, "What's gotten into me? How dare you! The real question is who did you snuggle up with last night? You two timer!" Instantaneously and inexplicably the five foot tall genteel female launched an unopened 5lb bag of Gold Medal All-Purpose Baking Flour. Butch evaded the powder-filled paper sack agilely. The millstone ground grain missile smashed against a wall and exploded like an atomic bomb at Los Alamos.

The next few seconds were literally a surreal blur. Mary's blowup dumbfounded Gavin and Sara. An obscure cloud concealed the perplexed pair completely. The kitchen was a zero visibility whiteout. Gavin gaped as the bleached wheat dust alit. His sister's shape corresponded Casper the Friendly Ghost's sibling. Butch and Mary also emerged akin to alabaster specters. Frosty the Snowman would've fit in nicely. The Pillsbury Doughboy may have panicked however. He might be on the pastry product hit list.

Gavin was delighted by the ludicrous extravaganza. Lunacy instigated his laughter. The chirpy child stuffed an immense piece of sandwich in his mouth. Gavin couldn't muffle merriment. He chewed and chortled convulsively. Butch applauded actively. The tardy husband who resembled a smart aleck albino Yeti teased Mary when he taunted, "That's one way to make our kitchen the antique eggshell color you've wanted." Butch wisely lunged outside. Mary slammed down an olivewood mixing spoon and chased the accused philanderer. Sara bawled until Gavin held her hand.

Mary's itinerary became busier. Every weekday morning she fulfilled the same routine fastidiously. The dynamo got out of bed, showered and put a robe on. Mary woke her children before she ushered them to the bathroom. Once hygiene requirements were sorted Mary helped the drowsy duo get dressed. The attentive caregiver prepared breakfast. After Gavin departed she donned work clothes and loaded Sara into an unblemished Ford Fairlane station wagon. The dedicated family cornerstone then drove towards Cougar Manufacturing Incorporated's facilities. Mary always passed Washington Elementary School and confirmed Gavin's bicycle was in a rack. The pundit presupposed his peers perpetuated truancy problems.

Women's liberation hadn't reached Hamilton. Mary's management of the firm was uncommon. She dutifully dealt with phones, requisitioned supplies, remitted bills, routed deliveries, processed invoices, compiled the company ledger, supervised Sara and reined in an impetuous husband. The titleless administrator functioned as Cougar Manufacturing Incorporated's Chief Operations Officer.

The detail oriented woman went home at 5pm. Mary had been on the go for twelve hours nevertheless she fixed dinner and bathed her children. The diligent mother made sure teeth were brushed. She then tucked both tired tykes into bed. Mary missed Butch and didn't sleep well.

Cougar Manufacturing Incorporated profits compounded. The organization was two and a half years old. Butch sported snazzy suits. His attire included Ray-Ban Wayfarer sunglasses and an Omega Seamaster wristwatch. The stylish wholesaler owned a car he preferred but previously couldn't afford. Butch parked an apple red convertible 1966 Ford Mustang in the company lot after he bought it and expounded, "To be successful you have to look successful." Mary suspected her husband had other motives.

Butch shared his affluence with his wife and children. The magnanimous man purchased a new powder blue Ford Pinto station wagon for Mary. Sara's doll collection multiplied and Gavin rode an iridescent yellow Sears Spyder bicycle. Relatives from Tennessee accompanied the Reynolds on a spendy vacation. The sightseers toured Glacier National Park and Alberta. They lodged at the Prince of Wales Hotel in Waterton, Canada.

Mary trusted her sacrifices were worthwhile. Every marriage has bumps. Butch sowed wild oats but the prodigal husband continually returned after he horsed around. Mary anticipated Butch would ultimately straighten up. An upbeat perspective bolstered the long game player's certitude.

Butch visited Missoula weekly. He intermittently met with a shady shyster who was on the city council. Doug Goldberg presided over three used automobile lots, two mobile home dealerships and an ignominious lending company. The diversified middleman also controlled less upstanding rackets anonymously. Butch and Doug were at the Edgewater Lounge when they encountered a Hollywood producer. The tanned sixty year old Californian had colluded with Doug for decades. An illicit arrangement led to the fictitious happenstance and a contrived confabulation.

The stranger shook Butch's hand. He obviously wasn't from Montana. Four diamond rings on the studio executive's soft manicured metacarpi gave his outlander identity away. The motion picture mogul wore an ostentatious orange leisure suit with a lavender polyester shirt. He had an impeccable smile that featured perfect pearly dentures. The silver screen maven sat down and solicited, "So my friend what's your occupation?" Butch tried to act casually. He self consciously confessed, "I manufacture pickup toppers."

After Butch's response the newcomer began devious deception. The showman smoothly stated, "My name is Samuel Silberstein. I'm a filmmaker." Butch succumbed to the conspiratorial character's charisma. Tinseltown temptations blinded the bumpkin. He didn't have an inkling of his plight.

The beguiled businessman amicably noticed Sam's empty tumbler glass so he tendered, "What are you drinking Mr. Silberstein? It's on me." Butch was a visual arts aficionado but he hadn't interacted with an illustrious luminary. The captivated pickup canopy purveyor signaled a cocktail waitress as he mused, "Maybe he knows John Wayne."

Sam's primary gift was his ability to sell second rate cinematography. He relied on two underwriter categories; crooks and chumps. Underworld mobsters who expected sanitized money comprised the first clique. Sam's X-rated sagas laundered their ill gotten gains. The pornographer's mafioso sponsors recouped investment capital and back end percentages from adult theater distribution deals. Sam's carnal coups were an avaricious criminal's dream come true. The duplicitous director had dozens of dirty dramatizations.

Star struck schlemiels were the second speculator group Sam targeted. The schemer defrauded merchants during erotic engagement interludes. It wasn't a crime when Sam scalped suckers because he always obtained signed contracts. The chiseler rendered footage his quarry funded but he drastically overcharged. Sam specialized in expedient commercials. The exorbitant advertisements filmed faster than an obscene movie. A speedy spell of skullduggery transpired before stooges debunked the dishonesty.

Doug and Sam were still thirsty so Butch bought another round. The Los Angeles swindler slurped an Old Fashioned while he plausibly legitimized his presence in Montana. Sam's full-length epic entitled *The Cowgirls of Anaconda* was delayed due to cast revisions. The hustler depicted a virtuoso as he further falsified. Sam deftly deceived Butch when he lamented, "It's too bad I have downtime. I wish something inspired my talents." Sam gestured both index fingers skyward and slyly cajoled, "I ordinarily don't do television but I'll make an exception for a resourceful young man like you."

Butch's vulnerabilities were exposed when Sam conferred, "The cameras, audio equipment, booms and my crew are here in Missoula. If you're interested I could provide an exquisite promo." The enticingly baited snare was irresistible. Butch consented to the bamboozler's provisos. Sam removed a production agreement from his briefcase. The ripoff professional clarified, "I only carry these silly formalities on account of our lawyers. Those putzs require legal documents."

Sam wielded an imitation Tiffany pen and filled in the document's blanks expertly. The crafty charlatan fleetly finished two carbon copy forms. Butch yawned and fidgeted. Sam astutely deterred his mark's reluctancy. The bilker unscrupulously assured, "This service commonly costs at least twenty grand." Butch signed the dotted lines and wrote a check for $9,500.00. The dodgy deal was done.

Mary and her children were in the kitchen when Butch arrived. The mass media tyro's entrance was unexpected. He briskly rushed through the back doorway. Butch sauntered across the linoleum floor and wrangled Mary's waist. The merrymaker foxtrotted with his wife like Gene Kelly as he exalted, "I've got big news!"

Sara mirrored her parent's animated movements. She stood on the chair and clapped in time. Gavin gawked at the gregarious gusto. He was disgusted by repugnant romantic revelry. The repulsed rascal retched like an alley cat as he grumbled, "You guys are gross."

Butch abruptly ceased his ballroom buffoonery with Mary and scooped up Gavin. He lightheartedly goaded, "You want gross. I'll give you gross." Mary grinned as she recovered breath. The astounded woman watched her husband waltz and gleefully interjected, "Butch you're too much. We can discuss it during supper." The debonair dad set Gavin down and hugged Sara. Butch went to the sink. He whistled "Singing in the Rain" and washed his hands

The Reynolds family sat at their kitchen table. Mary served one of her scrumptious single skillet Hamburger Helper delicacies as she requested, "So what's all this nonsense?" Butch beamed broadly. He swigged Dr. Pepper and disclosed, "Cougar Manufacturing Incorporated is gonna to be on TV. I'm telling you we've hit the jackpot."

Butch summarized the auspicious consultation with Sam. Gavin gathered his father had struck Hollywood gold. The gobsmacked child thought every entertainment industry idol was worth bundles. He hypothesized *The Beverly Hillbillies* were based on a true story. Grandma Kate's *National Enquirer* magazines delineated movie stars' luxurious lifestyles. Local sportscasters and weathermen undoubtedly lived in mansions. Gavin assumed the Reynolds family would enjoy analogous opulence. The naive visionary ventured, "We'll be rich and famous."

Mary disputed her optimistic son's opinion. The rationalist had seen an array of Butch's wayward whims. She brusquely stood and scoffed, "Here we go again. Another wild goose chase." Mary put her plate in the dish tub roughly. The miffed mother was peeved. She shook a rag and chided, "If you blow money like this Butch I will be forced to take the checkbook away. The bank manager has warned me about your shenanigans."

Butch feared his wife's cynical presence would corrupt Sam's creative process. The expediter diverted Mary with an excursion. He sent her on a three day Boise shopping trip. The fixer was flabbergasted when filming finalized in an afternoon. Ostensibly the talented actress went to Nevada because of other obligations.

A few days after the two man camera crew wrapped Butch inked an additional contract and post production was furnished for $2,500.00. Editing costs were not included in the original fee. When Butch scrutinized the extra expense Sam patiently proffered, "A secondary payment is standard."

Butch's advantageous activities resumed. Sam claimed he and an amenable Missoula television station owner were Alpha Mega Malaka fraternity brothers. The fraudster allegedly finagled affordable airtime. Sam boondoggled the brainwashed patsy blatantly. The misleading movie maker advised, "I talked him down fifty percent." Butch didn't read the fine print. He signed the binder blindly.

Sam fled two hours later. He flushed out five flimflams during a month-long artistic residency. Butch went home and imparted his fortuity. The capricious capitalist ardently described an unforeseen serendipity when he submitted, "I booked four half priced slots on KPAX. It's a steal." Mary couldn't resist an ironic rebuke. The clever conversationalist exercised sardonic sensibility while she snickered, "You're right Dear. It is a steal."

Broadcasts were scheduled for the upcoming Saturday. Gavin petitioned pertinent particulars when he entreated, "Why are you putting your company on television Dad?" Butch pondered his son's query. The mentor counseled, "It's to stir up interest so people buy more of our pickup bed covers." Gavin concurred with the sage assessment. He nodded and affirmed, "Pretty soon every truck in Montana will have one."

Gavin whipped up an illuminative public relations whirlwind. The propagandist enlightened classmates, teachers, bar patrons, store clerks and Ravalli Republic reporters repeatedly. He chattered constantly. The booster emphatically compelled, "Cougar Manufacturing Incorporated is on TV Saturday night. Tune in CBS at 10:40pm."

Butch took Gavin fishing the morning before his commercial aired. The angling buddies went to Aunt Ruby's homestead. Her Bitterroot River waterfront farm encompassed ten acres outside of Corvallis. The first rate fishermen caught six rainbow trout. Gavin then picked a puppy he would adopt after the floppy eared basset hound was weaned. The father and son extended their jaunt. They shopped at the Hamilton Packing Company indulgently. The high rollers procured premium hamburger, bratwursts and ribeye steaks.

At 5pm the Reynolds threw an inaugural telecast viewing party. Their debut gala kicked off with a barbecue. Gavin courteously greeted visitors. He supplied beverages and provided bug spray. Many mosquitoes were slain during the festivity.

Mary was an especially hospitable hostess. She dished up potato salad as women convened in the kitchen and second guessed her recipes. The accommodator graciously deflected derogatory discourse when females fomented a barrage of condescending commentary. Mary kept cool while the clucking brood inflicted their unsolicited guidance. The talented talker from Tennessee insincerely emoted, "I'm glad y'all are so helpful."

An ensemble of men surrounded a charcoal grill. The motley associates looked like hunched backed troglodytes. Butch flipped burgers, sizzled sausages and seared steaks while the Bitterrooters swilled beer. Politics were debated until proper subject matter prevailed. Farcical fabulist fishing fibs flourished.

Gavin was vexed because the soiree lacked age appropriate companionship. The bored kid heeded his mother's followup directive. Gavin safeguarded Sara while she played with an insipid Play-Doh Kitchen. The humdrum girl eschewed fascinating toys like ant farms. Gavin's ennui ended when Mary set condiments on the serving table and assigned her son a new task. She pleasantly instructed, "Sunshine please take your sister in the house to wash y'all's hands."

Shindig participants circled the bountiful buffet. Butch gave an amusing dinner prayer. He jokingly pontificated, "Lord bless this meal and a hungry flock of vultures who are here to eat on my dime. Amen." The convocation was reassured Butch's recent upswing hadn't made him an extremist. A lighthearted ambience arose. The assembly laughed raucously as they filled their plates with food.

The feasters' stomachs were stuffed. They retired to an uncluttered living room. Grandpa Joe sat in Butch's La-Z-Boy recliner and Grandma Kate seized Mary's Ethan Allen chair. Some well fed friends snagged sofa seating. Other socializers sprawled on the floor and used pillows as armrests. Everyone rejoiced when the Saturday Superstar Movie premiered. It was *Lassie and the Spirit of Thunder Mountain.*

Thirty five minutes into the cartoon classic Grandpa Joe snored and Grandma Kate wheezed as they dozed. Gavin fell asleep. When the ten o'clock news finished Butch gently nudged his son and murmured, "Hey buddy. Wake up." Gavin was stunned. A bunch of spectators were clustered around the RCA console's stupendous twenty seven inch screen.

At 10:30pm precisely *AWA All-Star Wrestling* came on. Gavin was aware of magazines that portrayed the glorious gladiators but he hadn't witnessed their colossal hand to hand combat. Expectations elevated when two grapplers entered the ring. Attendees were uninformed about Grandma Kate's proclivity for barbarity. They gawped while she heckled the Iron Sheikh. Grandpa Joe dejectedly sighed, "Men in tights. It just ain't right." He deplored televised violent villain debacles.

The Arab antihero was nearly pinned twice during round one. Incredibly the imaginative Iranian escaped via an illegal toe hold, ear bites and thumbscrews. The Middle Eastern maniac jeered while he pulled Dusty Rhodes' hair. When the diabolical genius stomped on his opponent's head with a curled toed boot Gavin became an evil emir fan. He studied the Persian master's torturous tricks intensely. The Farsi speaker's useful fighting moves were fantastic.

Three minutes of brilliant brutality broadcasted before the bell rang. The erstwhile world champion wrestlers went to their corners. Grandma Kate was livid. The grandmother who detested delinquents shook both fists as she squawked, "He's a hoodlum! The Iron Sheikh's an abhorrent rotten scoundrel! That cheating Tehrani troublemaker should be tarred and feathered!"

The awestruck audience muted. They were blindsided by the cranky busybody's flamboyant critique. Moods changed when a congratulatory crowd cheered her cantankerous caterwaul. Tomfoolery terminated after Mary implored, "Y'all hush. It's time for Butch's TV ad."

Cougar Manufacturing Incorporated's commercial commenced with an unhurried horizontal left to right pan shot across lodgepole pine trees until the camera froze and focused on a mist shrouded pickup topper. It floated magically in the air above an emerald green mountain meadow. The crimson pickup canopy majestically materialized as a tremendous treasure. An andante disco soundtrack reverberated.

The prized pickup topper hovered miraculously as a voluptuous vixen slinked out of an opaque fog machine background vapor. She sashayed in a sultry style and stroked the pickup canopy sensuously. The blond buxom beauty's struts stopped. Her hot pink fingernails rested on the flying phallic phenomenon's roof evocatively. The bra-less full figured forest fairy wore an airy gossamer beige slip and furry black stiletto high heels. A transparent skin colored negligee engendered an amorous illusion. The elf maiden with enormous mammary glands seemed like she was naked. At that juncture the shapely seductress's image enlarged. A close up accentuated the spokeswoman's anatomical assets. Two humongous hooters were highlighted. The curvaceous creature fluttered false eyelashes and performed an emotive Marilyn Monroe impersonation. She winked provocatively. The whispering well endowed pixie purred, "Cougar Manufacturing Incorporated. Toppers for the topless."

Suddenly the licentious vamp faded and round two tussles began. Nobody cared about the Iron Sheikh anymore. The stupefied viewers were confounded. It was surprisingly speechless until Butch stood up and soberly reflected, "We worked hard on the slogan."

A thunderous ovation erupted. Frivolity filled the room. Grandpa Joe wiped his teary eyes and brayed, "Yeah Butch. I bet you worked hard. Very hard." Uncle Steve amplified the hoopla and howled, "She's one cute kitty cat." Finally an insult was hurled when Grandma Kate cackled, "You really are the next Hugh Hefner."

Butch's annoyance was unmistakable. The irked ridicule recipient marched to his Ford Mustang and sped away. He imbibed at the Riverside Tavern until closing time.

Emily Post would've esteemed Mary's etiquette before the risque communique aired. The social event coordinator had exuded charm. Her kindly conduct corroborated congeniality. Mary's mellow mien manifested meritorious manners. Unfortunately self restraint was shattered as guests cracked jokes.

Mary faced the lampooners and loudly lambasted, "What's wrong with y'all?" She silenced the joyous jubilee. Histrionic yahoos mutated into somber skedaddlers. The tongue tied throng retreated rapidly. A discomfited ambiance ensued the disconcerting disaster.

Gavin went to bed. Mary hugged her son tightly as she consoled, "Goodnight Sugar. Your father and I love you." The baffled boy didn't acquiesce with his relative's hilarious hullabaloo. He couldn't unravel the commercial's adverse aftermath because of an indubitable fact. The memorable promotion accomplished Butch's intentions. "Toppers for the Topless" definitely stirred up interest.

Calls clogged western Montana's telephone network within moments of the tawdry testimonial's end. Bitterroot Valley party line brouhaha buzzed. Switch boards were swamped. Cougar Manufacturing Incorporated's thirty second spot was a spectacular scandal.

Reviews of "Toppers for the Topless" were divided. First Amendment defenders purported the monumental presentation defied unconstitutional censorship laws. Most women sanctioned an incompatible sentiment. Furious females called friends to fulminate ferociously about the filth.

Affronted phone callers inundated KPAX when the titillating telecast ended. Malevolent malcontents mandated permanent removal of the promiscuous performance from public airwaves. Brotherly compassion was spoken unilaterally. Harangers threatened to incinerate the station before they contacted

FCC officials. Distressed staffers capitulated and didn't rerun the indecent infomercial.

Various vehicles drove dangerously to KPAX's Regent Street parking lot. Three Missoula Police Department patrol cars swarmed towards the scene. An unnerved graveyard shift manager appeased rampant rioters. He carried the 16mm vulgarity outside and unreeled its spool into a metal trash can. Commotion enveloped him. An unruly mob chanted, "Burn that bawdy blasphemy!" The shaken supervisor applied lighter fluid, lit a match and stridently said, "It's not my fault." He set the advertisement's sole copy on fire. "Toppers for the Topless" flared up in flames.

Gavin eventually became an eccentric elderly citizen. Early one morning the grizzled grouser examined a photo taken at Lake Como in 1969. He recalled how his parents surmounted adversity. Mary and Butch somehow stayed wed for eighteen years. The couple confronted countless challenges throughout their marriage but they always prioritized progeny.

Time changes the way an individual looks back on past predicaments. Awful incidents like a "Gold Medal Flour Fiasco" and "Toppers for the Topless Travesty" transformed to comical anecdotes. When lifespans grow shorter bittersweet memories are frequently judged differently.

People say it's best to "forgive and forget." Gavin espoused forgiveness but he didn't agree with the adage entirely. The contrarian conjectured better advice might be "release resentment and remember." Family stories provide important parables. One notable moral teaches happiness and sadness are sometimes two sides of the same coin. Misfortune may morph into mirth. Gavin maintained mishaps can often activate amusement and empathy. Absurdity is an angst antidote. Embrace and sustain antic anecdotes whenever possible.

Giant Montana Pelicans

Kindergarten was Gavin's earliest exposure to a passel of peers. Socialization sprouted during the fall semester's first day. An irate classmate wielded a flyswatter and repeatedly bashed him. Gavin split his forehead on an ajar door as he eluded the angry assailant. A sugar cube soaked in Jack Daniels whiskey didn't alleviate cranial pain pulses. When the lacerated concussion recipient's mother showed up at Saint Francis's Child Education Center Sister Catherine de Medici apologized, "I'm sorry Mrs. Reynolds. Your son doesn't play well with others."

Gavin endured the introductory school year. Further hospital visits and stitches weren't required. The youngster's extraordinary academic advancement received an appropriate reward. A fantastic fishing trip was planned. Gavin and his grandfather would soon seek native bull trout in the tributary below Painted Rocks Reservoir Dam. Ravalli County locals called the lunkers dolly vardens. Many enormous behemoths swam in the Bitterroot River's headwaters.

Grandpa Joe looked like William Holden. He became an awarded B-17 bombardier during World War II. The Army airman circumvented capture twice when his plane was shot down. Parsnips and turnips were Grandpa Joe's only nourishment while he fled. The fortunate flyboy settled into a home outside of Hamilton, Montana. He detested most root vegetables and retired after two decades as an esteemed U.S. Forest Service employee. Leisure didn't suit Grandpa Joe so he worked part time at Red's Gas Station.

The mechanic was a leather skinned codger with countless crow's feet. He chain smoked Camel Straights and consumed coffee colossally. Gavin's toughened grandfather could be an irascible grump but he also retained a substantial sense of humor. Grandpa Joe grew up as an impoverished Great Depression child and served in a less than fifty percent survival rate squadron.

Gavin was startled when his father woke him at 5am. He glanced out an unopened bedroom window and detected headlights. The drowsy moppet derived, "Grandpa's Joe here." Butch put clothes on the bed and whispered, "Hurry now. Meet me in the kitchen." Gavin dressed swiftly.

The eager rapscallion sped downstairs, sat on a dining table chair and complained, "Why can't I take my fishing pole?" Butch handed his discontented son an iced maple cake doughnut as he replied, "Your grandfather has all the gear needed. Obey Grandpa Joe because he'll make sure you're safe. The river's upper west fork is extremely dangerous." Gavin gulped a mouthful of breakfast and answered, "I promise."

Butch ushered Gavin towards a white 1963 Dodge Dart. Grandpa Joe awaited alongside the vehicle. He danced an animated jig in the frosty gravel. Butch amicably announced, "Morning dad. It's kinda cold for late May." Grandpa Joe jocosely behaved like a battalion commander. The jester squinted at his grandson and chuckled. He authoritatively asked, "Are you ready to catch whoppers private Reynolds?" Gavin embraced the paragon and exclaimed, "Yes Sir!"

The adventurers shared an ardent country music affinity. They sang with Hank Williams, Merle Haggard and Marty Robbins during the drive to Darby. The dissonant duo dramatically delivered verbatim renditions. Grandpa Joe and Gavin flaunted flat key abilities. The tone deaf balladeers belted ditties until a weak AM radio signal dwindled. Grandpa Joe switched off the static and lit an unfiltered cigarette. The unmelodic minstrel exhaled smoke through a side window gap before he inquired, "Who's your favorite singer besides me?" Gavin didn't dawdle. The maven attested, "Johnny Cash tops my list. Dad says Charlie Pride played baseball and performed in Missoula bars. Could I really kiss an angel good morning?" Grandpa Joe coughed and responded, "It's possible. A cherub hugged me forty minutes ago."

An empty parking lot materialized when the expectant fishermen arrived. Gavin got out of the slant six automobile. A splendid environment enveloped him.

The wide eyed child's face dampened in an abundant mist. He was dumbfounded by the hoary surroundings. Gavin contemplated a crystalized shrub and silvery trees that shimmered. He peered at the phenomenal panorama. Rapids resounded so loudly the sidekick and his grandfather had to shout.

Grandpa Joe accessed the Dodge Dart's trunk efficiently. The expedition leader gave Gavin an Army rucksack. He assembled two salmon rods and handed one to his antsy assistant. Grandpa Joe unloaded a five gallon Shell Oil bucket along with an ammo canister. He closed the car trunk firmly. The odyssey orchestrator picked up his fishing pole, both repurposed receptacles and yelled, "Come on kid. Let's stake out a spot."

The anglers reached an overlook. Gavin hadn't seen anything like the powerful current. A cascade surged and churned through an elongated concrete walled channel. The astounded boy now fathomed why Butch warned him. A terrifying fact became obvious. The torrent would drown anyone who fell into its massive waves and undertows instantly. Gavin paused. The wary youth gazed at an upwell of white water worriedly. Grandpa Joe saw the distress in Gavin's eyes and grinned. He deemed the younger Reynolds spoiled their son too much. The savvy senior citizen maintained it was his responsibility to endow realities which built resiliency.

Grandpa Joe gripped Gavin's elbow and steered the uneasy child to a prime location. The site was fifty yards downstream from an inundated spillway. Gavin's grandfather set the steel pail and munitions case down determinedly. The skilled sportsman directed, "This is where we make camp." Grandpa Joe flipped the bucket over and advocated, "Take a seat." Gavin readily sat as he screamed, "The river's incredible!" Grandpa Joe beamed broadly and bayed, "I know. It's amazing."

Gavin was intrigued by the fishing pole he held. The curious grandson observed, "This rod seems strange. Why is it different?" The Reynolds cheaped out on trivial items but quality equipment was an essential priority. Accomplished anglers such as Gavin's grandfather understood proper paraphernalia fostered success. Grandpa Joe lit a cigarette and explained, "Fish are flushed into the river when engineers lower that floodgate. Huge trout stay beneath the chute. We use heavy duty 10ft Berkley poles with Shakespeare level wind reels and durable 25lb line."

Grandpa Joe prolonged the demonstration as he instructed, "Scoot over. I'll show you an effective rig setup." Gavin moved the bucket closer. Grandpa Joe unlatched the ammo box. He extracted a mini tackle kit, an 8 oz Folgers Coffee can, two rod holders and his hatchet. The outdoorsman noticed Gavin's shivers. He astutely suggested, "Take that aluminum thermos out of my pack and pour yourself a cup of cocoa." Gavin implemented Grandpa Joe's advice. The tyke drank Swiss Miss gratefully.

Hypothermia was averted and the lesson resumed. Gavin focussed attention as Grandpa Joe threaded an antique cork bobber while he unreeled nine feet of line. The nimble fingered fisherman secured a bullet lead sinker and attached an Eagle Claw #3 steelhead hook. Grandpa Joe inspected the Palomar knot intently. He gave Gavin his other fishing pole and proffered, "You can prepare this one. Show me how it's done." He supervised as the student added a bobber and sinker. When Gavin tied an Improved Clinch knot on the hook Grandpa Joe complemented, "That's outstanding." The masterful monitor then remarked, "Hey kid. Help a feller out." Grandpa Joe tossed the crusty coffee can to Gavin. His coordinated grandson unsealed the container and enthusiastically exalted, "Nightcrawlers. Awesome!"

Gavin impaled earthworms on both barbs while Grandpa Joe pounded two stick rod mounts into the soil with his small axe. The sunny gorge warmed. Dawn's emergence from darkness reminded the former aerial combatant of life's preciousness. He savored an exquisite vista. The Ravalli County resident rejoiced, "There's nothing like Montana!"

Grandpa Joe retrieved a fishing rod. He prudently expounded, "Sorry kid. I'll do this part alone." The capable caster neared an oxidized railing. Gavin's grandfather catapulted the wiggly worm in one fluid motion. The graceful man's arm dexterity rivaled Johnny Unitas. Grandpa Joe floated the baited hook into a teeny eddy. He activated an 8lb reel drag and placed the pole inside a ground spike's cylinder. The agile angler proved his first effort wasn't an accident. Grandpa Joe skillfully hurled the supplemental line even farther. He maneuvered his bobber to a gentle whirlpool, adjusted drag settings precisely, put the rod in its holder and humbly concluded, "Couple of fluke casts. Now we wait."

And wait they did. By 10am the inauspicious fishermen hadn't gotten any bites. Gavin was bored until Grandpa Joe opened the waterproof holdall and proposed, "I'm peckish. Perhaps an iron ration picnic is in order." He dispensed saltine crackers, cheddar cheese and smoked sardines smorgasbord. The pitiful piscators finished their fine snacks. Grandpa Joe looked at his watch and propounded, "Guess we're not going to have any luck. Let's get on our way home."

Militaria fascinated Gavin. Thirty minutes into the trip towards town he speculated, "Those aircrafts you flew in were cool." Grandpa Joe abruptly reduced the radio's noise. He pulled to the roadside and stopped. The dewy eyed veteran stared somberly as he contended, "A lot of my friends died in Europe. War's the worst thing people do. When an Army GI's dead he doesn't come back. I hope you'll never fight in battles."

The rapt youth listened as Grandpa Joe continued, "Do you remember your scared reaction at the river this morning? When my plane was in a dogfight that's how it felt. Guys who say they're fearless are liars." The psychologically scarred ex-serviceman blew his nose with an old bandana and advised, "We should grab grub." Gavin appreciated Grandpa Joe's ample appetite. The bottomless pit for a stomach scamp submitted, "I could eat an entire pizza."

Gavin watched Grandpa Joe's tears as the conversation ended. He now ascertained why the sporadically sorrowful hero was granted miscellaneous dispensations and what Grandma Kate meant when she urged, "Go easy on your grandfather. He's broken up inside."

Grandpa Joe increased the radio decibels and drove away. Roger Miller's "Dang Me" sounded from a Delco dashboard speaker. The grandfather and grandson hollered like two intoxicated hillbillies while they howled along with chart toppers. Regrettably Aunt Ruby's basset hounds missed the outrageous operetta. Her deranged dogs would've fit in. Jerry Reed's "When Your Hot, Your Hot" created an uproar. The throaty tenor and strident soprano crooned raucously as Jimmy Dean's anthem "Sixteen Tons" began. George Jones' "White Lightning" generated clamorous caterwauls. The off pitch misfits parked in Hamilton and Grandpa Joe yodeled, "Hello Darlin'. Nice to see you again." Gavin didn't unravel the joke until he saw a curvaceous eatery server.

The troubadours strolled to an immaculate counter. Grandpa Joe sat at his standard spot and Gavin hopped on a stool beside him. An attractive waitress in a maroon plaid uniform acknowledged the cohorts charmingly. She carried an aromatic carafe and flirtatiously queried, "Good afternoon Joe. Who's the handsome stranger?" Grandpa Joe winked as he drawled, "Hi Trudy. This is Gavin. He's my grandson and a mighty hungry fisherman." The bleached blonde poured her regular customer an inky cup of coffee. She set the pot onto a burner, took out an order pad and averred, "I suppose you want your usual." Grandpa Joe was gentlemanly when he respectfully requested, "Yes Ma'am. Make it double. The kid looks thirsty. Could we please get a root beer?"

Trudy sauntered to the refrigerator and came back with an open soda pop bottle. Grandpa Joe sipped coffee. He then questioned, "Do you approve of bacon sandwiches?" Gavin nodded as his tutor opined, "Restaurant etiquette is important. I normally purchase a BLT and soup. If an establishment can't cook that meal they wouldn't be in business. Always act politely and leave a hefty tip. It pays off. Ladies like Trudy will occasionally provide an on the house pastry." Grandpa Joe gave Gavin two quarters and recommended, "Pick out some songs."

Hopefully heaven is similar to Cafe 93. Its exterior resembled Seattle's Space Needle top section. The delicious food diner had a red, black and polished chrome Art Deco design. Downrod etched glass pendant lights illuminated the bright bistro. Plush booths featured Formica tables and miniature jukeboxes. The devices communicated with an orchestrina that played 45 rpm vinyl records. Gavin was a Wurlitzer wiz. The maestro found an acclaimed tune his grandfather favored before he pushed B and 3 buttons. Patsy Cline's version of "Crazy" resonated richly.

Gavin chose five more hit singles, returned to the counter and wolfed down lunch. The pint sized disc jockey appealed for guidance from his grandfather as he muttered, "Have you ever been in a wedding?" Grandpa Joe supplied an absurd statement. He jocularly informed, "That's what they called it when I married your grandmother. Indentured servitude is a more accurate description." Gavin huffed and moped. The grumbler disclosed, "My parents say I gotta be an idiotic ring bearer. Last time I stood up in front of people it was a failure."

The protester previously discovered his theatrical improficiency subsequent to an infamous incident. He blundered amidst the Eagle's Lodge *Winter Holiday Pageant*. Mrs. Fitzpatrick was the production's director. She accommodated Gavin's script memorization inability and assigned him a solitary line. Sadly he stammered, "Behold! We are Three Wise Men from...er...Bozeman!" Gavin's mistake instigated an ebullient ovation. Despite audience approval a few straightlaced censurers construed the Nativity scene shouldn't be comical. They demanded the novice thespian's demotion. His wool allergies were ignored. Gavin enacted an aphonic sheep role morosely.

Grandpa Joe recognized Gavin's perspective. The grandfather deplored public appearances. Regardless of his opinions the sensible confidant encouraged attendance when he counseled, "Banquet chow is tasty. You should go." Gavin grimaced. The pessimist was reluctant. Grandpa Joe attempted to ease resistance. He sincerely reassured, "You'll do great."

Trudy refilled Grandpa Joe's java and giggled as she quipped, "This dapper youngster deserves huckleberry cobbler with vanilla ice cream." Gavin heeded his mentor's earlier pointers after he devoured a delectable dessert. The protege petitioned, "May I borrow twenty cents for an excellent tip?" Grandpa Joe was amused. He smiled and stipulated, "Let's make it a dollar." The well fed gourmands paid before they ambled outside. Rain started to sprinkle. Straightaway the summer storm catalyzed an earthy scent. The Bitterroot Valley atmosphere permeated a perfumed paradise.

Grandpa Joe brought Gavin home and parked the Dodge Dart. He handed the Army rucksack to his grandson. The generous grandfather meaningfully mentioned, "Take this backpack. You need it more than me." Gavin held the treasure tightly. He was overwhelmed. The elated youth affectionately extolled, "Thanks Grandpa Joe!"

Gavin's trip to the matrimonial rehearsal duplicated an inscrutable seminary symposium. His brain ached when the Reynolds arrived at a Baptist Church in Missoula. Mary had demystified dissimilarities between Catholic belief system credos and the bewildering basilica's ethos. Gavin garnered an emphatic Cross Sign gesture while he articulated, "In the name of our Father, Son and Holy Spirit," was strictly prohibited by this peculiar parish. The confused catechism practitioner grasped genuflection germinated disapproval. Coincidentally the uncanny cathedral's congregation didn't anoint with Consecrated Water or constantly cry for clemency. After Gavin learned the enigmatic sect eschewed confession he contested, "That's unfair."

A portly preacher greeted the Reynolds. Gavin deduced Mary's monologue omitted an imperative detail. It quickly became evident there were various types of priests. Gavin hadn't encountered a parson like the red haired reverend who wore an aquamarine blue suit and sported silver clasped white pleather loafers.

The plump pulpiteer could've been Jerry Lee Lewis's corpulent cousin. His gold ringed manicured fingers glittered. Butch was shocked when the buck-toothed ecclesiastic shook hands and spewed, "Howdy folks! I'm Pastor Jim! Welcome to our Redeemer's residence! Right this way!" Messiah's messenger seated the flabbergasted family in a first row pew. The Creator's considerate child plodded away as Butch griped, "Gosh darn evangelists."

Protocol practice went smoothly. The hormonally unbalanced female fiancee only erupted emotionally seven times. Participants perspired profusely pursuant to three hours preparation. The worship chamber lacked climate control. Everyone was pleased when the afternoon finalized with Pastor Jim's oral affirmation. The sermonizer stated, "Dear spectacular Savior. Bless this blissful betrothal. We also celebrate your divine dispatch of the Reynolds into our faithful fold. Help these corrupted Catholics repent. Amen."

Butch stomped from the sweltering tabernacle with Mary and Gavin in tow. The miffed man slammed his family's Ford Fairlane station wagon door before he growled, "That guy has an awful lot of nerve." Mary appeased her choleric husband. She rolled down the passenger window and consoled, "I'm glad you were diplomatic. The bride's prestigious. People say Jennie Swenson's dad might run for governor." Butch lit a Pall Mall cigarette and admonished, "I don't care. On Saturday we sit in the back benches."

Mary lightened the situation when she diverted discussion topics. The mollifier asserted, "Let's pick up food from that new place with yellow arches. We can eat on the way home. Connie has babysat Sara for hours." The Reynolds stopped at McDonald's. During the excursion towards Hamilton Gavin bellyached, "Why do they cut icky onions in such tiny pieces? I scraped that yuck off of my burger and it still tastes horrible." Mary endeavored to placate her unhappy son. The mindful mother handed him an emulsified proprietary chemical laden soft-serve chocolate concoction and comforted, "Here Sweetie." Gavin slurped the straw. He pouted and criticized, "What kinda lame milkshake is this? I'd rather have a root beer float."

The Reynolds revisited Missoula two days after they tolerated fake flavored frozen beverages. An onerous drive transpired during the hottest temperature on record for western Montana. When the four family members motored through Woodside crossing Gavin scratched maniacally. His pristine nylon fiber clothing was intensely itchy. Butch drove past Florence and the future ring bearer's skin festered. Gavin's mostly black attire made him wonder if the ceremony had been changed to a funeral.

Another problem Gavin suffered was the apparel's snugness. He usually donned weathered jeans and loose t-shirts. The stiff synthetic weave pants forced him to strut like an austere sentry at Buckingham Palace. Gavin agonized acutely. He thought the title "slacks" incorrectly defined his clingy trousers that chafed.

Gavin's draconian footwear inflicted torture. The Buster Brown Oxford shoes bred blisters. When the inflammation victim reached Lolo he presumed his raiments provided a procedure for pitiless pious Protestants to punish prepubescents such as himself.

Butch parked the station wagon and escorted Gavin into an office that served as a dressing room. When they trotted inside the discombobulated boy saw five fidgety men. The agitated associates were clad in ivory hued jackets with baby blue bow ties and cummerbunds. Gavin perceived the party plainly parodied an apprehensive pod of penguins. The gangly groom was named David Jensen. He brandished a garment bag and implored, "Here's your son's outfit. Have him ready in ten minutes."

Humidity hovered in the cramped room. Butch sweated copiously and began to dress Gavin. The perplexed youth was dubious of cummerbunds so he surmised, "Girdles are for girls!" Butch stuffed Gavin into an undersized topcoat. The contorted child's scarecrow arms stuck out sideways. He could barely bend the blazer's inflexible sleeves that bound both biceps. The petulant imp evaluated his predicament and apprised, "This stupid suit strangles. I walk like Frankenstein."

Gavin had a thick neck. The uppermost button transformed shirts into an asphyxiation inducing tourniquet that impeded carotid artery blood flow. When Butch cinched Gavin's bow tie the grievous boy gasped, "That terrible elastic chokes like a noose." David Jensen tried to calm the cantankerous carper. He patted Gavin's back and conferred, "It's okay pal. Formal wear is always uncomfortable."

An acrimonious accusation ensued. Gavin didn't comply with the incomprehensible logic. He resented the groom's consultation crossly. The irritated sourpuss disrespectfully decried, "I feel like there's a rope around my throat. Is that why an imbecile gets hitched when he ties the knot? I hope Pastor Jim doesn't moonlight as a hangman." Butch discerned Gavin's disaffection but he was delighted due to the derogatory dig his scion distributed. The proud dad tittered quietly and posited, "It'll be over soon. You look sharp."

Physical and mental breakdown loomed. The suffocating sportcoat simulated an asylum straight jacket. It caused a claustrophobic effect. An alarming tempest brewed with dehydration, oxygen deprivation and stress. The captive ring bearer verged hyperventilation when he begged, "I want to go home." His plea for liberation went unheard. The line between Gavin and institutionalization in a psychiatric ward was razor thin.

Additional difficulties tormented Gavin. The rattled rascal carried an azure pillow with two platinum rings attached to it during his awful aisle amble. He accompanied a gigantic girl dressed in an irradiant sky colored gown who scattered flower petals. Attendees were distracted by rose fragments when Gavin reeled and careened. The lightheaded lurcher teetered like a disorderly drunk. He ascended an elevated altar and almost dropped the minuscule cushion.

Gavin's surreal spell sustained on the dais. A dizzy distorted sequence mirrored Salvador Dali dream depictions. The flustered boy swayed beside an oblivious groomsman. He witnessed four women bouquet holders that wept woefully. A pink baptismal hot tub undulated in tempo with Wagner's "Bridal Chorus." The torrid temple's thermometer exceeded one hundred and eight degrees.

Pastor Jim commenced the obligation oath oration. Gavin hushidly mumbled an incoherent Hail Mary mantra. The herky jerky hallucinator gesticulated uncontrollably. Assorted nuptial onlookers sensed stagefright afflicted the spasmodic six year old. Gavin's boa constrictor bow tie and cruel collar ensemble wrung his windpipe. Vertigo entranced the breathless whippersnapper. Disorientation engulfed him as the ordained emcee emoted, "If anybody objects to this virtuous union speak now or forever hold your peace."

Gavin verified the slogan "Weebles wobble but they don't fall down" was a myth. The unsteady urchin emulated Humpty Dumpty. When he upended the precious cerulean satin covered pillow and both rings launched. The high velocity projectiles landed near rear row pews. An octogenarian expressed disbelief with a profound profanity.

Although nobody boomed "timber" Gavin approximated an inclined ponderosa pine felled by a woodsman. The rigid swooner slanted when he tumbled backwards. Several gasps reverberated while the plunger performed an inverse swan dive. Gavin espied a kaleidoscopic swirl as he turned topsy-turvy and plummeted off the podium. His cranium impacted the orange carpet violently. The incapacitated juvenile blacked out.

An Olympic Judge would've given Gavin's glorious feat a perfect score. The confounded crowd cringed in unison. Suddenly the stunned spectators were concerned. The cursed Catholic child triggered trepidation. An exorcism of the Pope's possessed emissary was probably necessary. Pastor Jim briefly beheld a tremendous theological crisis until he confronted the Satan influenced circumstance courageously. The proactive clergyman cawed, ""Hallelujah! I now pronounce you husband and wife."

Pastor Jim diligently discontinued the disquieting disaster. An abbreviated culmination occurred forthwith. The seasoned salvation spin doctor exhorted, "Praise Jehovah! These disciples of the Divinity may kiss!" He rapidly cued the organist. She played Mendelssohn's classic "Wedding March." The Almighty's ambassador hadn't ever presided over a chaotic calamity such as Gavin's demonic dilemma. He was perturbed about legal ramifications. The Lord's shepherd hastily herded an anxious assembly away from a potential wrongful death investigation sight.

Gavin and his father were the only oratorium occupants. Murmurs emanated from the vestibule. Butch mercifully removed the jacket, cummerbund and bow tie. He unbuttoned the shirt's garrote neckband.

Saint Raphael came to Gavin's rescue. The audacious acrobat awakened. Butch was relieved. He uttered, "Hey Buddy are you alright?" Gavin groaned groggily. The woozy failed ring bearer sat up and slurred, "What happened?" Butch's exasperation expanded. He plied an ecru linen handkerchief, gently dabbed the casualty's brow and avowed, "Enough is enough. We're done with this debacle."

The frustrated father and convalescent son trudged toward fresh air. Butch gave Gavin's rental garb to a deacon as they exited the edifice. The disgruntled dad met his wife and daughter. Butch inconspicuously insisted, "We're outta here." Mary was disinclined. Exclusive socialite repasts were rare for the erstwhile sorority officer. She obstinately objected, "My Lotta Enchilada Casserole is on the serving table."

Butch scowled and discretely made his point. He subtly hissed, "I'll buy you new Corningware. It's cheaper than Missoula jail bail." Mary accepted Butch's ultimatum and acquiesced. She carried Sara to the family vehicle without further contention.

Gavin and Butch sought to sidestep Pastor Jim when they left the erroneous espousal. Unfortunately the rabid revivalist intercepted both ineffectual evaders. Butch halted before he courteously reasoned, "Gavin's still pretty sick. Goodbye and godspeed." Yahweh's yapper persisted with his pejorative platitudes. The pesky pontificating proselytizer professed, "Thank our King of Kings. The little devil's okay. Would you consider an insignificant contribution to our sanctified sanctuary's Community Fund? A diminutive donation ensures prayers for your misguided souls."

The impertinent idealogue's impudent insult ignited irascibility. Butch couldn't turn the other check anymore. The principled debunker revealed revulsion when he snickered derisively. Butch glared at the wolf in sheep's clothing indignantly. The fired up Franciscan furiously fumed. Butch castigated the impious charlatan as he contemptuously snarled, "Pastor Jim. Pray for an air conditioner. It boiled like fire and brimstone in the building today. Cooling systems are quite costly. You'll need a thousand gullible tithers. Sorry us poor Catholics can't afford to emancipate you from that hellish inferno."

Butch's tirade silenced Pastor Jim. The voiceless vicar stood slack jawed. When the Reynolds sped away Butch sighed deeply until he exulted, "It's an astonishing miracle! We escaped that atrocious ordeal. Who wants A&W!" The Hamilton papists parked at their favorite drive-in restaurant. Butch placed an immense order.

Gavin ingested a Papa Burger and recalled Grandpa Joe's comments regarding reception edibles. The fast food fanatic's meal was undoubtedly superior to puritan potluck pabulum. He pertly proclaimed, "I bet the Baptist buffet doesn't have French fries."

KYSS radio station entertained while the dogans dined. Aretha Franklin's "Respect" and John Denver's "Rocky Mountain High " were joined by an inane trio. Sara clapped along with her farcical family. A commercial broadcasted and Butch decreased amplification. He realized Mary hadn't heard his tongue lashing of the money motivated minister. When Butch wrapped up the report he hooted, "That Bible thumper's facial expression was priceless. There's an extra special Hades for hypocrites like him." Mary supplied syrupy sarcasm. The witty Tennessean declared, "Bless Pastor Jim's heart."

The Reynolds enjoyed joviality and their scrumptious dinner. They then drove south on Highway 93. When their automobile crossed the Buckhouse Bridge Mary shrieked, "Pull over! I see a giant Montana pelican." Butch had read an article about the birds that nested at Arod Lake. He promptly parked atop the pavement's shoulder. Butch got out, loped around the station wagon and opened both side doors briskly. The attentive father assisted Gavin as he argued, "Are you certain it was a pelican?" Mary debated her husband's skepticism. The slighted woman scoffed, "I'm positive. I saw them in Florida."

Butch clutched Gavin's hand as he neared the span. Mary toted Sara and trailed closely behind. The Reynolds reached an unimpeded vantage point. They stopped and surveyed below. A cryptic creature waded through an idyllic deep water pool. Nobody deciphered the fabulous figure. Butch solved the mystery when he whooped, "I can't believe it. It's a topless temptress in the stream. I'm glad we get to spend time with Mother Nature."

Gavin's peepers bulged like an Amazon tree frog as he ogled at the bare breasted maiden. She rode a somewhat submerged Appaloosa filly. The naked equestrian's torso and her horse's head exhibited an optical effigy. They actually mimicked a humongous Pelecanus.

Mary identified the skinny dipper and squawked, "Don't look! An indecent nudist is on a nag!" In spite of her rebukes Gavin gawked at the siren's B sized bosoms. Butch chortled convulsively and buckled in half. Hilarity enthralled him. The ludicrous laugher blurted, "It's not an American pelican but I think that critter's definitely related. She's the most beautiful booby bird in Bitterroot River history!"

Gavin hoped the giant Montana pelican anecdote would be retold. Fifty four years after the escapade he took a teenage grandson fishing. The two generations sat on Bayview Jetty while they ate rye crackers, feta cheese and smoked salmon. Gavin spotted flocks of brown pelicans so he recounted Mary's legendary avian sighting. The narrator completed his tale and postulated, "We're catching more sand fleas than flounders. Time to go."

The hapless anglers proceeded to an ancient dented Plymouth Valiant. Gavin conveyed knowledge as he said, "We're a weird wonderful family. Never forget you're part of this kooky clan. Ancestors dwell in our memories. Keep their stories alive."

The Ravalli County Rebels

An enigmatic girl named Brenda Boyd began to attend Hamilton, Montana's Washington Elementary School. She was the only second grade newcomer when fall semester classes started. Gavin Reynolds felt a strange sensation in her presence. The beguiled Bitterroot Valley boy had an extreme case of romance. He naively disseminated hormonal histrionics. His unprecedented passion presented plentiful problems.

The susceptible seven year old quickly comprehended amorous affliction consequences. Gavin's cute classmate rejected a relationship. The earnest Romeo's amicable efforts induced loud admonishment. Brenda became an enraged banshee when she browbeat the smitten sap with shrill rebukes. The diva's debasement developed as her devotee's desire deepened.

Gavin mistakenly divulged the crush condition to his friends Mike and Danny. They constantly teased the confused Casanova. One day during lunch Mike pointed at Brenda while he heckled, "Gavin's captivated. The kook's crazy." Danny accompanied Mike's denouncement. The wisecracker cawed like a Blue Jay and cackled, "He's infected. The dunce's got girl germs." Gavin resented the condescending cohorts. Amore wasn't an amusing topic for ridicule. He curtly exclaimed, "Shut your yaps."

Every time Gavin neared Brenda a formidable force enveloped him. The bewitched boy postulated she was an apprentice sorceress. Her incantations mutated Gavin into a bundle of nerves. Whenever the bonehead beheld Brenda he spluttered untranslatable guttural syllables. Even though the articulate kid generally enunciated eloquently Gavin blurted Paleolithic phonetic phrases such as "Ugh, Ugh, Ugh."

Brenda's scorn perpetuated. She pelted Gavin with an icy slush ball amidst a January recess. The soaked suitor ogled at Brenda while slurry oozed down his neck. She wore an artificial fur coat and could've been a Whitefish Winter Carnival Junior Princess. The splendid snow sphere hurler strafed spectacularly. Brenda had an arm major leaguer stars would envy.

When Gavin gave Brenda a Valentine's card she dropped it on the ground and sneered, "What an idiot." The disdainful dreamboat then haughtily strutted away. A view of an immense purple comb that bounced in her rear pocket eased Gavin's embarrassment. The lascivious voyeur drooled. He gawked and muttered, "She's so hot." Danny heard the simpleminded statement. He smirked and spouted, "Brenda's right. You're a dope." Mike summed up succinctly. The synopsis specialist joked, "He's an asinine lunatic."

Gavin alleged adoration and abhorrence were the closest emotions. He explained the oxymoron during a sleepover. Danny and Mike listened while the logician extrapolated Brenda cloaked her fervor with fury. His heartthrob acted repulsed but she actually adored Gavin. The infatuated idealist clarified an irrefutable irony as he avowed, "It's called reverse psycho activity. Sometimes people say the opposite of what they really feel. When Brenda screams hatefully it means she yearns for me. Any shrink doctor would tell you the same thing."

A second grade picnic was held on the school year's last day. Gavin and his pals ate ice cream sandwiches while the sentimentalist wistfully emoted, "Brenda will miss me. I hope she comes back in the fall." Mike nudged Danny and winked whimsically. The prankster interjected, "Go ahead Gavin. Give her an affectionate farewell kiss." Danny appreciated the provocation Mike provided. He flapped his elbows like wings. The comedian coerced, "I double dare you." Danny and Mike clucked raucously. The rowdy duo resembled Rhode Island Red roosters.

Gavin couldn't forgo the challenge. His extortionist buddies' blackmail was unbeatable. The brash boy capitulated. He had no choice because only doofuses ducked out of double dares. Gavin preposterously proclaimed, "I'll do it."

The brave buffoons skulked warily towards a gaggle of girls who were congregated next to an unoccupied swing set. Gavin approached Brenda from behind and tapped her shoulder. The acrimonious young lady's giggles ceased. She twirled around and contemptuously hissed, "Don't touch me you creep!" Gavin suddenly stuttered a sentence. The fallacious fantasizer mumbled, "I dink I loaf do." Gavin puckered and laid his lips on Brenda's left cheek.

Considerable conversation circulated about the epic event that ensued. All Gavin recollected was his eyesight disappeared. When the smoocher regained consciousness he saw an azure sky and a huddle of faces. Gavin groggily groaned before he asked, "What the hey?" Mike and Danny helped the smackaroo deliverer stand. It took minutes to clear countless cobwebs. The canoodler's woozy head wagged continuously until he questioned, "Did Brenda slug me?" Gavin's friends jovially recounted the single punch boxing bout's gory glory. Both compatriots enlightened the amnesiac while he recovered.

Gavin compressed an ample paper towel wad to quell his bloody nose. The flummoxed fall guy moaned, "Brenda's not a boxer." Gavin's compassionate caretakers confirmed his consternation when Mike consoled, "Her fist floored you like Ali decked Jerry Quarry" and Danny sympathized, "That hook reminded me of Joe Frazier." The osculator 's right cheek discolored as his swollen eyelid turned dark purple. Polite bystanders labeled it an insignificant contusion but even Gavin recognized Brenda gave him the biggest shiner in school history.

Vice Principal Wagner hand delivered a written communication to the families involved that afternoon. His resolute findings related, "Brenda justifiedly resisted Gavin's lechery. While Washington Elementary School discourages violence an exception is warranted." The official mimeographed document mentioned, "Brenda properly pummeled the masher who mauled her. The valorous girl's retaliation was valid. All accounts vehemently verified Brenda's appraisal when she towered over the comatose cad and shrieked, 'You're a perv!'"

The appalled administrator's rigorous dispatch noted, "Gavin slurred, 'I coo do loafed me.' He then crumpled in an ugly heap at Brenda's feet. The deviant's deplorable personality disorder should be thoroughly evaluated." Mr. Wagner's write-up concluded, "Warm Springs Mental Hospital treatment is available." The bruised boy incurred less rigid rehabilitation. Gavin's guffawing father grounded him for two weeks. The offender was instructed to meditate upon his birdbrained blunder and its unwelcomed reception.

Gavin repented after repeated remonstrations. He endured extra chores and limited privileges. The reformer's promise to never peck without permission prevented psychiatric therapy. His punitive mother ensured the ungentlemanly urchin learned an unforgettable lesson.

Brenda Boyd indoctrinated allies. When September came she led a gang that rode pink bicycles with tasseled handlebars. Her cruel clique could've starred in the 1968 classic *She Devils on Wheels*. Brenda's colleagues were the town's four fiercest third grade girls. Derision was the predatory pack's primary weapon. They wielded it skillfully. The inhumane harassers hunted heartlessly. Meek young men avoided the malevolent merciless matriarchal mob.

Intimidation emitted from Brenda. She chomped grape Hubba Bubba and issued an array of iniquitous commands which would make Catherine the Great tremble. The hellcat maintained a Farrah Fawcett inspired red mullet. Brenda walked, talked, chewed gum and feathered her hair simultaneously. Girls revered the powerful phenom. Boys lived fearfully. Brenda was the school's alpha female.

Classes hadn't begun on the fall semester's first day when Brenda's spiteful squad encircled Gavin, Danny and Mike. The savage stalkers converged as their bellwether imposed an undeniable dominance. Brenda pointed at her prey while she snapped, "Lookee here. It's the Perv and his clueless cronies."

The moniker Brenda gave Gavin flourished. Her callus coven clamored the sobriquet whenever they saw him. Most students didn't speak the slander receiver's real name. He was referred to as "Perv." Even Danny and Mike addressed Gavin with the epithet. His companions also regaled in roundhouse wallop reminiscences. The raconteurs frequently reenacted Brenda's prominent pugilistic performance.

Gavin grew up in a generation whose physicians recommended bottle fed infants. Breasts baffled him. Virtually everything the youth ascertained concerning feminine anatomy was garnered from an explicit nudist river sighting and Danny's ransomed Sunset Malibu Barbie. A monumental metamorphosis transpired the evening his father's pickup canopy company aired an indelicate television commercial. It featured a "Toppers for the Topless" slogan and an alluringly clad Marilyn Monroe lookalike. Before Gavin espied the spokewoman's stupendous cleavage he didn't fathom how gigantic a lady's mammaries could be. The imp believed Barbie's beau Ken belittled buxom bosoms.

When Gavin arrived at school after the raunchy telecast flooded Montana airwaves he was oblivious to its public prestige. The uninformed cyclist parked at an empty bike rack. Mike moseyed over, held up his right hand and urged, "Give me a high five!" The greeting committee's enthusiastic commentary carried on. Danny slapped palms with Gavin and congratulated, "Far Out!"

Gavin doubted the unusually warm salutation. He tentatively inquired, "What's the big deal?" Mike lauded the crude commercial's momentous merit boorishly. The frenetic fan of indecency flicked his fingers and announced, "That nearly naked lady on TV's legendary. She's an icon."

The honoree temporarily enjoyed eminence until his nemesis interceded. Brenda Boyd prowled towards Gavin, Danny and Mike when the bell beckoned children to classrooms. She loped like a lioness. Her ferocious friends followed. Dr. Pepper Lip Smacker Lip Gloss aroma and angst filled the air ominously. The inert boys abstained eye contact while they contemplated retreat routes. Fight and flight weren't options so the pals stood in an instinctive self defense triangle.

Brenda prepared to pounce. She separated the herd and isolated its most vulnerable individual. The vicious virago snarled, "Hey Perv. Your father's a sicko pornographer!" Her accusation was artful and advantageous. Gavin approximated an Easter Island statue. A Spaghetti Western movie soundtrack suited the spectacle. Brenda blew an enormous bubble and popped it before she growled, "This sleaze is a scumbag. Gavin's the son of an icky sex addict. He's a Perv's Perv!" The clangorous castigation crescendoed as Brenda's accomplices converted into an ear-piercing quartet. A crowd gathered while they robustly recited an obviously rehearsed refrain. The femme fatales repeatedly roared, "Gavin's a Perv's Perv!"

Caterwauls hushed and Brenda abandoned her adversary like an appeased feline in the Serengeti. She pretentiously purred, "Come on girls. We don't have time for these dorks." Mike and Danny emulated tongue tied ostriches. If the sensible sidekicks had been able to they would've buried their heads. When the fiendish females were beyond earshot Mike declared, "Geez Louise." Danny was shaken by the skirmish. He shivered and stammered, "That monster's a menace." Brenda's aggressive attention dazzled Gavin. The spellbound schoolboy whispered, "She's magnificent."

Brenda's animosity prevailed until the third grade year culminated. She tormented the wooer tirelessly. There was an inventive humdinger among her vindictive coups. A "secret admirer" gave Gavin an innovative donkey themed card. The meaningful memorandum's read, "Dear Smelly Mule. Roses are red. Violets are blue. If you love Brenda you're through." Gavin defied the veiled warning and his adulation abided. Brenda's vengeance persisted vigorously. The absurd symbiotic interdependence became a wellspring of widespread Bitterroot Valley gossip.

Summer break after third grade began with an unsupervised boon. A fabulous freedom was found as Gavin, Mike and Danny marauded. The masterless anarchists spurned hierarchy.

Mike made plans to rectify the leadership void expeditiously. The megalomaniac contended an autocratic chain of command would yield better raid results. He also wanted power. The despot dreamed up a club concept during an allegorical motion picture rerun. Marlon Brando's *The Wild One* role stirred Mike's action.

The most essential quality for prospects of Mike's organization to possess was fortitude. All other traits were negligible. He devised a hazardous scheme that assessed mettle. Survivors would be an intrepid faction who knew the group's motto. Only the elite could become a "Ravalli County Rebel."

Mike's opportunity came one late June morning. The arranger glanced out an uncurtained living room window. His buddies' bicycles were beside Mr. Gelato's market. He scrambled outside as Gavin and Danny egressed the neighborhood deli. They compulsively consumed candy bars. Mike cantered across Main Street. He brandished a comb and slicked back his greasy flat top hair. Mike vocalized an incredible Fonzie Fonzerelli impression. The lampoonist's timbre was identical to Henry Winkler when he drawled, "Ayyy. How's it hangin'?"

The audience was tepid at best. Gavin unwrapped a Baby Ruth and complained, "Aw shucks. Our moms have jobs for us. It's an unfair case of exploitation." Danny avidly bobbed his noggin. He didn't favor child labor either. The jocular juvenile masticated a Mounds mouthful and lamented, "I don't get paid."

Mike had readied an underhanded ploy. The tactician resolved to catch a couple of lunkheads so he contrived an effective strategy. Mike used a bait and switch technique. The con artist cast an initial lure as he confided, "Chores. Too bad. Guess you weaklings will miss out on a terrific chance."

Gavin reacted like an excited brown trout that sensed a stonefly larva. He couldn't resist. The impulsive imbecile rashly jabbered, "Miss out on what?" Mike snagged the hook and began to reel Gavin in. The story spinner then contributed an irresistible enticement as he tempted, "It's not much. Me and some subversives started a covert club. I thought you clowns might join." It didn't take long for an additional bite. Danny swallowed the falsification and entreated, "Groovy. Can we enlist after our gruntwork?" Mike set the second barb.

Cognitive agility was crucial to dupe two chums conjointly. Mike finessed the flippity flop friends superlatively. The manipulation master cleverly furthered fraud as he fibbed, "Our meeting will be postponed but I'll accommodate you guys."

Mike had completed the conclusive step of his dastardly deed deftly. The creative controller snookered Danny and Gavin. It was simpler than he envisioned. The smug string puller silently opined, "Those nitwits are suckers."

Gavin and Danny hurried home. They met in the backstreet between their houses a few hours later. Gavin was wary of Mike's intent. He nobly notified, "That joker's shifty." The crackerjack cyclists raced away.

Danny and Gavin sped stridently. The zippy pair pedaled like amphetamine crazed hamsters during an antidepressant pharmaceutical experiment.

Both speed demons decelerated behind Mike's garage and heard a hammer. It banged intermittently. When Gavin and Danny rounded an alley side building corner the noise paused. A roller door was open so the bike riders parked. They witnessed their host. The clumsy carpenter squeezed an indigo colored left thumb and quietly cursed, "Dagnabbit." Mike eyed the arrivers before he pocketed his mangled manacle. The habitual hematoma hider casually commented, "You dweebs finally made it."

Gavin acted cool. The posturer cleaned his teeth with a cinnamon toothpick and displayed disinterest as he scrutinized, "What kind of moronic club did you hallucinate?" Mike matched Gavin's acrimony. The devious negotiator shrugged and replied, "You're probably too wimpy to be in an outlaw gang."

Danny contrasted the combative counterparts. He didn't disguise his gusto. The candid madcap petitioned, "What's your coalition called?" Mike snorted derisively. He was insulted by Danny's impropriety. The pompous pendant lambasted, "You pantywaists haven't passed a mandatory membership initiation test."

Gavin grimaced, whirled around and faced Danny while he yelled, "I told you he has an ambush." Mike was well acquainted with his cynical censurer. Once again he taunted to secure compliance. The oral orchestrator prodded, "Gee whiz Gavin's gutless. Real renegade outfits don't let cowardly jerks join. There's always a jump in tryout."

Mike's audition nettled Gavin. He assumed the brotherhood typified his Grandpa Joe's adage, "If something seems too good to be true it stinks." Gavin's hostility heightened because Mike had gotten him into repugnant repercussions previously. The devout pessimist was disgusted and expressed contempt as he criticized, "You're full of booger snot."

An intervention took place when Gavin marched out. Danny galloped past the provoked pal and placated, "It can't be that horrible." Mike also detained the deserter. He trotted outside and goaded, "He's not tough enough." Gavin wrinkled his brows. The rankled dissenter grudgingly consented due to peer pressure. He sourly surrendered, "I'm in."

Mike brought hammers to Danny and Gavin. The untrained builders inspected a half baked bicycle ramp. After the boys settled specifications they pounded nails abysmally. The woodworkers uttered clean cusses such as "dang, fudge and Jiminy Cricket." Discretion hampered requital. If Mike's mother eavesdropped swear words her reprisal would be severe.

The pseudo profanity pontificators finished their crooked assemblage. Mike's sister delivered Kool-Aid to the thirsty crew. Three cherry flavored drinks were savored before Gavin evinced an inconsistency. He incredulously accused, "Why aren't the other club guys here?" Danny hadn't caught onto the discrepancy until Gavin's insinuation. He cantankerously chipped in cross-examination and concurred, "Yeah. Where's your weirdos?" Mike concocted a pretext. The artifice aficionado artificially admitted, "Those yellow bellied chumps didn't qualify."

Gavin was frustrated by his friend's chicanery. The straight shooter shouted, "Cut the crud Mike." Danny voiced exasperation likewise. The riled recruit huffed and demanded, "What are we supposed to do?" Mike disregarded the pugnacious pals' descent. He seized the wooden slope and snarkily stipulated, "You ladies will see soon."

Bicycle ramps were the exalted recreational hobby for Bitterroot Valley boys that summer. Older fanatics jumped dirt bikes, dune buggies, cars and trucks. The daredevil king was an indomitable stuntman from Butte, Montana. Evel Knievel's death defying motorcycle exploits on ABC's *Wide World of Sports* incited awe. Mike venerated the celebrity's credentials when he affirmed, "He's broken every bone in his body."

Evel Knievel's wealth was earned unconventionally. He commenced freelance endeavors with prosperous rackets. Evidently the sheriff didn't approve of enterprising delinquent teenagers. He banished Evel from Silver Bow County. The exile enlarged his entrepreneurial empire. He became the second most famous person on earth. Only Muhammad Ali surpassed Evel's stature.

Folks claim monetary rewards are based on success. Evel established the premise's inaccuracy after his first professional crash. When Evel visited a promoter's trailer he was persuaded to jump again the following day. Rumors spread about his smashup. Fairgrounds stands were filled before the next appearance. Evel landed and swerved into barrier hay bales. The motorcycle madman received an opulent bonus.

Evel diverted his destiny. He figured there was a cash cornucopia in defeat. Damageless extravaganzas decreased attendance numbers and television ratings. Evel discerned people paid pretty pennies to watch wipeouts. The public craved crackups so he satisfied their hunger for havoc. Failure financed the Knievel dynasty.

Much to Ravalli County women's annoyance the high-flyer's fame was compounded locally. George Hamilton's biographic film *Evel Knievel* screened at the Roxy Theater as an eight week Saturday Matinee. Admission, a small popcorn and soda pop cost one dollar. Showings sold out recurrently. The cinematic triumph also headlined Starlite Drive-In Motorcycle Movie Marathons.

Danny, Mike and Gavin worshiped the idiosyncratic idol. They cited his wisdom constantly. Evel Knievel t-shirts, trading cards and Stunt Cycle toys topped birthday wish lists. Each boy rode an adapted bicycle. The motivated associate's modified choppers were tours de force. Mike's garage was used when the munchkin mechanics toiled on customized creations. The ingenuous trio rebuilt cruisers with banana seats, long forks and slanted handlebars. Their good bikes were bad.

Gavin and Danny relaxed after the ramp was positioned. The capable cyclists conjectured Mike's challenge would be a cinch. They portrayed proactive perspectives. The composed candidates were stunned when Mike added complications to an already audacious audition.

Both aspirants eyeballed the plywood gradient and Mike pestered, "Hey twerps. I'm not done with details." The abominable architect dragged a hay bale while he informed, "Evel Knievel doesn't just become airborne and land. He soars over obstacles. So are you bozos." The contestants stared at Mike's sadistic artistry. Danny mused as Gavin hollered, "Freakin' flim flam!"

When Mike put his hay bale lengthwise against the incline Gavin calculated necessary trajectories. He computed the distance would be difficult but it was doable. Gavin patted Danny on the shoulder and assured, "We got this." Mike sniggered in an eerily deranged fashion. The sly caper coordinator scoffed, "You ninnies ain't got nothin'."

Mike went to the garage and returned with two thirty gallon plastic bags that clanked loudly. The sinister torturer scowled like Snidely Whiplash. He poured approximately one hundred beer cans onto a now treacherous landing zone. Mike beheld the masterpiece before he taunted, "If you cry babies survive you've got enough grit to be in my gang." Gavin and Danny gaped. The gobsmacked duo deduced Mike had given his subterfuge scads of dedication. They were the unprincipled choreographer's pawns.

Wreck probability expanded exponentially and Gavin's infuriation intensified. Mel Blanc would've complimented his conniption fit. The bitter boy groused, "What in tarnation are those cans for?" Mike's sardonic snicker tingled spines. The shenanigan savant submitted, "It'll make an eruption of sparks when you land."

Mike flipped a Buffalo Wooden Nickel and it was ruled Danny jumped first. The tow headed scamp soon straddled his bike at an impromptu starting line. He hoofed like a berserk bull. Danny concentrated with potent purpose. He reversed his hunting hat to improve aerodynamics. Gavin rooted for the courageous comrade as he cheered, "Hang in there Danny!" Mike raised an unwashed red bandanna and bellowed, "Three! Two! One! Go!"

Danny vamoosed valiantly. The plucky prodigy accelerated and discharged dust. Danny mobilized momentum. His eyes bulged bigger than a bushbaby. He rocketed forward and was five feet from take off. Danny confronted gravity. He hit the ramp dauntlessly. The tires' impact thundered. An amplified boom best described by the word "Wham!" resounded.

The lionhearted leaper launched and utilized Evel Knievel's style. Danny stood as he flew. The acrobat's midair bicycle yawed. Danny corrected his flight path before he executed a touch and go on the hay bale gracefully. The nimble navigator glided beyond every can.

Danny alighted and propelled onward. The screwball was so overwhelmed with relief he didn't stop. Danny bustled for forty yards and applied the coaster brake in an impressive rooster tail skid. Gavin sprinted to the unharmed cyclist. He slapped his gallant ally's back and whooped, "Outta sight!" The plauditory pal's forceful whack triggered Danny's turbulent tummy. He turned a putrid green. The nauseated youth helplessly heaved and projectile puked. An arched vomit surge nearly sprayed Mike. Danny's spew stream exploded on the ground. A splatter pattern comprised of peanut butter, Wonder Bread, raspberry jelly and an Almond Joy encrusted the gravel.

Mike was perturbed. The stickler protested, "That doesn't count. He missed the cans!" Gavin defended the upchucker's achievement. He glowered and barked, "I quit if Danny failed your stupid tryout." Mike tolerated Gavin's ultimatum. He begrudgingly relented, "I'll overlook it this time." Mike diffused empty beverage containers to maximize a catastrophe chance. The discontented doom dealer derided, "You're next sissy boy."

An anxious ambience loomed. Gavin simmered at the starting line. He adjusted his Hamilton Broncos baseball cap and dime store sunglasses. The daring dimwit gripped his handlebars tightly. Gavin was miffed. He wanted to thwart Mike's diabolical ruse. The aggravated avenger grievously grumbled, "Goldurn gopher droppings."

Danny munched on a Milk Dud while he bolstered his feisty friend. The nonstop chocolate nosher exhorted, "You can make it Gav." Mike's goals were converse. The scoundrel coveted cataclysmic calamities. He held the handkerchief flag aloft and bayed, "Ready! Set! Go!"

Gavin burst ahead like Speedy Gonzales. He hustled and hooted, "Arriba! Arriba! Andale! Andale!" The spunky rider zoomed at supersonic velocity. Gavin's bike blasted across the ramp. Plyboard buckled briefly beneath the breakneck bicyclist. He vaulted from an imploded wood surface. Bliss overtook him and a majestic moment materialized. Unfortunately an awful disaster detonated when the misguided marvel came back to earth.

Reverie terminated as Gavin alit. His two wheeler slammed down and plowed through cans explosively. The aluminum cylinders similarized shotgun shell pellets. Gavin lost control when the rear rim spokes collapsed. The contortionist slid and careened until a deflated front tire torqued perpendicular to an intact bike frame. Gavin catapulted horizontally. He somersaulted and his buttocks bashed the ground. Pebbles scattered profusely.

Danny and Mike aped ambulance technicians. The misfit medics approached a macabre accident aftermath promptly. They were unprepared for grisly carnage. The rescuers lacked duct tape, an emergency first aid kit, Ringer's Lactate and a gurney. Gavin wheezed and coughed before he proffered, "Gadzooks!" Thankfully the bungler was alive. If he had died his mother would've slain everyone involved in the fiasco.

Harsh reality was revealed when Mike and Danny assisted their buddy while he arose. The buoyant banterers howled like hyenas because of Gavin's shredded trouser tush section. An unmistakable road rash covered the kid's keister. Danny couldn't contain his chortles. The punster presented pitiless platitudes as he quipped, "Dude. You've got a bum rap." Gavin's ordeal overjoyed Mike. His comprehensive apocalypse transcended prognostications. The mayhem maker commended, "Radical ride Gav. You dipsticks can join the club. We're the Ravalli County Rebels."

Gavin's adrenaline dulled as aches agitated. Agony and delirium magnified. The casualty's teeters rivaled an imbibed tavern regular at closing time. He stumbled to a twisted jumble that once was an awesome bicycle. Gavin's backside throbbed while private parts pulsated. The unwell whippersnapper's rock embedded left elbow bled. Gavin staggered and reeled. Danny grabbed the lurcher's right arm. He worried about the wobbler's welfare. Danny exhibited sympathy. The somber pal posited, "Are you okay?" Gavin's stupor had subsided somewhat so he answered, "Yeah I guess."

A gambit germinated. The cunning cabal fashioned an applicable fabrication to fool authorities. Many moralists deem such behavior as blameworthy but for the abettors it was a frequent modus operandi.

Gavin's laceration liability obliged him to stretch the truth. Mike presumed his disheveled friend needed an explanation when he went home. The fanciful fable adherent foresaw potential ramifications and implored, "If our parents hear how Gavin got hurt he we'll all have a sore behind."

Mike avouched an alibi was imperative so he drafted a plausible scenario. Logging trucks played an important role in his duplicitous depiction. The masterful fixer disclosed a prudent proposition subsequent to an interval of rumination. Mike dispensed a revised anecdote as he directed, "Gavin tell your mom an insane lumberjack almost killed you."

Danny, Mike and Gavin's conspiracy began. The complicit collaborators tidied alley evidence. They shoveled a bevy of fly infested barf blotches under bushes and dispersed blood stains with an archaic hoe. The scene sweepers used a leaf rake to hide tracks. After tire tread marks were expunged the clandestine colluders concealed ramp remnants and Gavin's bent bike beside Mike's garage. The camouflage connoisseurs' countermeasures evaded detection.

Mike invited the initiates to an inane induction ceremony. Danny and Gavin affixed lickable Jolly Roger buccaneer tattoos before the sociopathic systematizer supplied "Keep on Trucking" patches. Mike then demonstrated the bona fide fraternal handshake. He spat in his palm and bestowed high fives. The commander flaunted superior intelligence when he conveyed a confidential code. It was the profound phrase "our password is password." The ritual adjourned with an axiom that plagiarized Evel Knievel's credo. Both probationers held up saliva coated arms as they vowed, "Bones heal, pain is temporary and chicks dig scars."

The new Ravalli County Rebels plodded towards their houses. Gavin was dismayed. The limper realized he embodied a blockhead who repeated errors and expected different results. Mishaps continually forced the melancholic kid to deceive. Gavin dreaded his imminent dishonesty. The wounded waif looked at Danny and sniveled, "Fiddlesticks!"

Gavin's mother disbelieved the demented timber truck driver drama decisively. The naysayer reprimanded her son's recklessness. She grounded the Mercurochrome recipient for one week. Gavin insisted he was irreproachable throughout his incarceration.

Danny sought recompense. He impelled the narcissistic club president to make an apology. During the first meeting after Gavin's parole Mike conceded, "I'm glad you're not maimed permanently." The prideful pal didn't recant but reconciliation came. Oftentimes Mike's deeds meant more than his words. The stubborn chum gave Gavin wheels, slightly worn tires, inner tubes and a set of forks. Mike scavenged the components off discarded bicycles he dismantled. The faithful friends relinquished grudges. They embarked on an infamous crusade.

A club gathering eventuated the next day. Danny debuted an avante-garde attitude. He wore a sleeveless ripped jean jacket with the "Keep on Truckin " patch safety pinned onto its right pocket. An old aviator's helmet covered Danny's cranium. Peter Fonda's *Easy Rider* influenced the character study artiste's demeanor. He duplicated Dennis Hopper mannerisms but his garments accentuated a do it yourself design. Danny swaggered into the garage and cockily imparted, "I'm hip man." Gavin's bike repairs took an entire afternoon. The bloody knuckled boys worked while they brainstormed revolution. A mere six band aids were pasted on.

The Ravalli County Rebels explored Hamilton's alleys. Myriads of mementos manifested. The repurposers modified an inoperative baby carriage to manufacture a trailer. Club policies vacillated but the gleaners never stole acquisitions. Cast off collections were the harvester's main source. They salvaged what was destined for landfills. The recyclers amassed an extraordinarily doodad caboodle.

Mike's garage was no longer a suitable headquarters. The obsolete objects amalgamation spawned backlash. Pryers were irritated about the ambitious association's gargantuan cache and carped cholerically. The rubbish reapers roamed until they scouted four closely spaced cottonwoods that provided an ideal place for a treefort. An immediate move to the drained swamp followed forthwith. The hoarders relocated a humongous conglomeration. An incompletely assembled elevated structure stood when July ended. A hobo camp motif replicated Fred Sanford's decor philosophy faithfully.

The rambunctious Montanans refined rummaging repertoires. Scientific forays replaced random sorties due to an unforeseen situation. The bounty reclaimers encountered a bonanza at an expired surgeon's manor. Medical gadgets were maneuvered while Mike asserted, "This croaked guy owned swell contraptions." Danny didn't disagree. He donned a stethoscope and surmised, "Apparently dead people get rid of goodies because they don't need them." Gavin's imagination illuminated. The insightful analyst sapiently observed, "I bet stiffs have nicer junk than everybody else."

Gavin's theorem underwent evaluation. The bright boys read obituaries and reconnoitered cremated corpe's homes. Estate sale's leftovers provisioned an educative plethora. The cadavers jettison superb debris hypothesis was corroborated after a few expeditions. Consistent results proved top notch troves proliferated in postmortem digs. When the perspicacious party probed daisy pushers' properties another inkling actualized. All quests indicated affluent goners generated stellar artifacts. The selective statisticians edited demographic data and pursued rich extinct bigwigs' refuse. Precision patrols to purloin the privileged passed away populace's paraphernalia were prioritized.

An aged magistrate kicked the bucket during August's third week. The shrewd scourers lurked in shadows as his brick abode was emptied. Mike surveyed the activities and commanded, "We meet tomorrow morning by the geezer's trash cans before any garbage trucks come."

A perished Justice of the Peace plunder proceeded proficiently. The Ravalli County Rebels were punctual. They rode to the deceased judge's domicile at 8am. Only leather bound statute tomes remained. Mike was disappointed so he squawked, "There's nothing here but an anthology that smells like moth balls."

Danny bypassed his bellyaching buddy. The erudite fostered a fondness of intellectual edification. He perused an antediluvian volume and adduced, "It's legal statutes. They'll be handy if we have a run in with the cops." Danny loaded texts into the retrofitted buggy. It was attached to Mike's bicycle. When the club leader noticed Danny's cargo he yawped, "I ain't towing those nerd weights. Hook the hauler on your bike." The squabblers squared off. Danny accosted Mike's admonition. The academia advocate defiantly argued, "You're an obtuse oaf!"

Gavin ignored the bickerers as he sifted a barrel. The gifted sorter wore gloves due to an odiferous dog poop debacle. Gavin suspended the inspection when he saw a peculiarity. The fleet fingered archeologist procured an unblemished brown paper parcel and pivoted towards his fractious clubmates. They tussled while Mike unknotted the trailer hitches. Gavin impatiently berated, "Why don't you wiseacres quit goofing around? I found something." The antagonists' altercation halted abruptly.

A meticulous munitions maven would've respected Gavin's exactitude. He fastidiously laid the anomaly on an upended fruit crate. The reliable retriever gingerly unfolded a grocery bag. Gavin's phantasmic psyche paralleled an eager prospector's gold fever. The waste bin enthusiast speculated, "Maybe I discovered a million bucks." Mike dealt deliberate denunciation. The muckraker mocked, "It's probably worthless Confederate currency." Gavin opened the sack and scanned inside. His grin gleamed as he crowed, "We've struck paydirt!" Danny and Mike peeked at the precious package.

Euphoric elation infused an ebullient Ravalli County Rebels hullabaloo. Jubilation burgeoned boisterously. The red faced confidants chortled gleefully. Danny danced a jaunty jig and Mike hopped like an elated wallaby. The roisterer rejoiced, "A nudie magazine!" Unity was unanimous. The thrilled trio celebrated their unequaled breakthrough until Gavin gloated, "We're not going to need Sears catalog bra sections anymore."

Mike predicted underage girlie gazette holders might be stopped and searched without Miranda rights recourse. Ergo he adamantly circumvented accountability. The onus eluder pointed at his patsy and prescribed, "Finders are keepers. Possession being ninety nine percent of law means Gavin carries the loot he dug up." The surreptitious sneak secured an adequate stooge. Mike preserved pretend purity if the provocative publication pirates were taken prisoner.

Gavin fulfilled Mike's decree. He sealed the bag and put it in his Army rucksack. The steamy journal bearer briskly scrammed. Danny was mesmerized by the magazines and transfixed with wide mouthed stupefaction. A ribald revelation enraptured him.

Mike peered at Danny's pathetic plight. The peeved policymaker pedaled past his paralyzed pal while he ordered, "You're an imbecile. Get out of here!" Danny obeyed the demonstrative dictate. He rallied rapidly and swiftly strapped two wagon tow bars to his bicycle.

Danny left the inanimate adjudicator's former dwelling as he raved, "Wait for me!"

The Ravalli County Rebels fled. When the evasionists arrived at their partially constructed clubhouse they dismounted and dashed into a wigwam. An asymmetrical willow tree raftered the brush blanketed hut. Optimism ballooned as the inquisitive boys sat near a legless end table. Danny activated an irradiant flashlight and held it under his chin. The wacky wit used a Count Chocula accent while he ventured, "I vant to see smut." Mike furnished frivolity. He clicked on an electric torch and facetiously requested, "Unveil the undressed!"

Gavin unpacked the prized parcel from his backpack. He unfurled the paper sack and removed two magazines. The periodical purveyor warned, "Keep your mangy mitts off this stuff." When the diligent debauchers' lamps lit each publication exuberant exhilaration emanated. Handel's "Hallelujah" befitted the occasion.

The first magazine was a March 1966 issue. Its cover illustrated an intriguing winterscape that mirrored a *Rudolph the Red-Nosed Reindeer* still frame. The image represented an erect eared and bow tied white rabbit snow sculpture. A skimpily attired foxy female figurine leaned against the handsome hare. She modeled an orange, cream and crimson knit cap. A color coordinated sweater hardly hid her hips. The erotic sprite sported thigh length black stockings and fleecy slippers.

"Entertainment for Men" was printed above the trophy's title. *Playboy* magazine's price appeared on the right hand corner. An affordable payment of seventy five cents provided a tremendous value. Mike, Danny and Gavin reckoned benevolent benefactors printed the economical monthly as an amiable nonprofit. A bottom page blurb promoted Ian Fleming's unpublished adventure *Octopussy*.

Further fascination followed. The second bawdy bulletin showed an enchanting young woman who outshined a Miss America Pageant participant. She wore an attractive big bang bouffant beehive hairstyle and gazed with impish emerald eyes that shimmered playfully. The pixie's pearly toothed smile was flirtatious. A glove puppet supported her adorable face. The charming cutie created an amazing paradox. She epitomized maidenhood and a mischievous mantrap mutually.

The March 1970 issue featured an exceptional "Nine Page Pictorial Spread of Rising Star Barbi Benton." Gavin, Mike and Danny reviewed the gorgeous brunette's portraits attentively. The curvaceous creature was flawless. Gavin supplanted his previous obsession when he doted on the delightful damsel. Brenda Boyd didn't matter anymore. The ghastly girl's magic mojo vanished. Her nefarious powers were quashed. *Playboy* publications liberated the priorly possessed prepubescent.

Both magazines highlighted other Playmates. Tantalizing tableaux documented dozens of furry booted nymphs that frolicked in a frozen fairyland. Every snapshot produced an exhaustive discussion regarding the vibrant voluptuous vixens' various virtues. Piquant panoramas might have been photographed at a Bitterroot Valley naturalist's resort such as Sleeping Child Hot Springs during December.

The periodical's founder exemplified refinement when he shared an enriched frosty utopia. His brilliance was relished by many. The publisher's proponents included a lifeless judge and three Hamilton chums. Gavin approved of *Playboy's* chief executive. The backer babbled, "Hugh Hefner should run for U.S. President."

After an ardent research session the boffins made a critical decision. The magazines couldn't be stored in their leaky hovel. Element exposure already destroyed an extensive catalog collection. The unfinished tree fort lacked two walls and a roof. An arid locale was necessary. Only one alternative to shelter the taboo glossy treasure existed. A dilemma debate developed. Which Ravalli County Rebel would take the lurid literature home with him?

Unbelievably Mike instigated an empirical solution when he suggested, "One of us needs to stash the magazines. I say we draw straws." The coincidence sustained a complementary serendipity. Mike kept three

Montana Cafe chopsticks in his daypack for such an impasse. He fetched the fate determiners instantly.

Mike held the wooden utensils in plain view. The misdirection maestro rationalized, "These are ordinary chopsticks. The short one loses. Danny will hold them while we draw so you're sure it isn't a trick." Mike gave Danny the food picker uppers as he averred, "Gavin can choose first. That eliminates funny business."

Gavin detected Mike's insidious antics but how could the scammer cheat when he didn't control chopstick disbursal? The credulous cretin purported his odds were enhanced because he had leadoff turn. Gavin hesitantly accepted Mike's recommendation as he yammered, "Get it over with." The boys chose. Gavin obtained the diminutive dowel. He was the perplexed and vexed victim of an unscrupulous Three Card Monte scam variation.

Mike owned the *Amateur Magician's Handbook*. His amoral hoax was very simple. A miniscule pinhole identified the smallest chopstick. Mike selected second therefore at least one unmarked Asian cuisine apparatus remained in Danny's grasp. Either Gavin or Danny acquired the little chopstick. Mike couldn't lose.

Gavin shouldered the scapegoat responsibility reluctantly. The bamboozled buddy sullenly specified, "I'll take the *Playboys* home. My mother's nosy. She'll find the magazines if I keep them too long." Danny's mindset corresponded. He acutely advised, "Let's finish the tree fort tomorrow." Mike also endorsed schedule amendment. The assenter remarked, "We rendezvous here at 9am."

Gavin never fully construed his inability to mislead. Quite simply he wasn't an accomplished charlatan. The inept prevaricator's guises were easily exposed. Gavin whistled nonchalantly when he carried the contraband into his house. Mary stood at the stove and descried her son's eccentric conduct. The tenacious woman's keen sensory radar equivocated a mother grizzly bear. She smelled the pheromone of fright. Mary quizzically queried, "What's new Sweetie?"

Ad lib encumbered Gavin. The untalented actor didn't anticipate his mother's waylay. He carelessly volunteered, "I need to write an important report." Mary's amiable approach outperformed a good cop during an interview. The confession extraction expert demurely expounded, "Well Darlin' it's summer vacation. Why do you have homework?" Sweat beaded on Gavin's brow and his ears rang like fire alarm bells. All the predicament missed was a spotlight. An additional falsehood emerged as he substantiated, "I want a head start." The salacious courier scurried upstairs. Gavin's dodgy deportment denoted deceit and an unconvinced Mary intended supplementary interrogation.

The magazine smuggler's blood pressure skyrocketed. Gavin entered his room and closed the door. He laid the backpack on a nightstand. The apprehensive boy was positive his mother would visit so he pulled an encyclopedia out of a writing table drawer and simulated scholarly activity. Gavin tried to calm down. His panic riddled brain blared, "Think! Doggone it! Think!"

Gavin sought an optimal site to secrete the parcel safely. The anxiety sufferer studied his surroundings. There was no convenient cranny. Gavin neared hysteria. He panted and perspired prolifically. The troubled tyke teemed with trepidation.

After Gavin reevaluated the closet, desk and dresser he was desperate. The pinup publication plotter prayed to Saint Christopher. Providence blessed him. Gavin withdrew the grocery bag from his canvas military holdall and tucked it under a twin sized mattress. He straightened the covers just before Mary knocked.

Gavin feigned an interruption while his mother invaded. Mary carried two Twinkies and a glass of milk. The information seeker's bribes implied she was on her son's side. Mary served the snack and offered, "Hey Sugar you look tired." Gavin nodded as he internally reflected, "You're not going to trip me up."

Mary appropriated Gavin's tote. The steadfast snooper connoted, "This knapsack's filthy. I'll wash it." She unceremoniously dumped the backpack's contents onto an empty bedspread. Candy wrappers and two comic books fell out. Mary examined the evidence as she slyly entreated, "Do you have anything else that's dirty?"

Gavin motioned mutely. In accordance with laws against self incrimination the perpetrator shook his skull sideways. Mary clutched Gavin's confiscated carry all and exited another inquisition episode.

The game of cat and mouse continued. Gavin aspired to limit dialogue whenever possible during dinner. His quiet comportment confounded both parents. The chatty child hadn't spoken a word. Mary's inflamed intuition increased while the reticent rascal ignored Hamburger Helper Lasagna. Gavin's reduced appetite was atypical so he griped about an achy stomach and excused himself from the table. When Mary rinsed the dishes she chronicled Gavin's awkwardness to her husband. The dubious mom enjoined, "Keep tabs on that boy Butch."

Gavin was surveilled the next morning. Mary monitored her son's every move. Transport of the prurient periodicals would inevitably be intercepted. The rattled rapscallion decided to leave both magazines in his bed. Gavin finagled authorization when he mendaciously professed, "Is it alright if me and the fellas go fishing?" Mary presupposed Gavin's absence facilitated a fine tooth forage. The wily woman acquiesced, "Sure Snookums. Y'all be careful."

Deer Lodge State Prison guards were novices compared to the Montana matron. Mary excelled at search, seizure and retribution. She attested her investigations of Gavin's illicit inclinations benefited the greater good. Crimes required reciprocity. Comeuppance cultivated redemption. Guilty parties must atone for their own best interest.

Mary inferred Gavin's culpability but the sleuth lacked proof. When her son skedaddled she hastened upstairs to his room. Mary methodically mimicked an engrossed bloodhound. Nothing was amiss until Mary scoped the sole place she omitted. The meddlesome mother lifted Gavin's mattress and a condemnatory paper aberration appeared. Mary's misgivings multiplied.

The bike ride mollified an iota of Gavin's turmoil. He approached the tree fort and saw his clubmates. The belligerent builders personified tetchy Tasmanian devils. They had installed a wall before the spicy publication paladin rode up. Danny was crabby due to Mike's constant critiques. The irked artisan squinted down from above and propounded, "This klutzy clodhopper works like an orangutan." Danny's derogatory defamation fomented the feuding friends' fracas.

Gavin parked his bicycle as he apprised, "My mom badgered me at breakfast and I couldn't bring the *Playboys*. I told her we're fishing so I'll have to amscray early. If I return without trout she'll be suspicious."

The trio strove for six hours. Danny nailed the last piece of plywood and fastened a roof tarp. He watched as Gavin pedaled away. The morale booster emphatically encouraged, "Keep calm and carry on!" Empathy wasn't Mike's forte. The egotist blustered, "You better bring back those Playmate pictures!"

Gavin detoured an overfished stretch of the Bitterroot River. He angled at a three foot wide irrigation ditch. The location was classified. When cars passed the resourceful kid disguised his aquatic avocation. Gavin pantomimed an aimless ramble along a road that abutted the tiny channel. He didn't deploy an actual fishing pole. The precocious piscator used a monofilament line and an earthworm baited hook. Gavin caught five fat brookies adroitly.

The adept fisherman proceeded home. Gavin parked and went inside. Mary was in the kitchen. She glared sternly. The livid lady chastised, "Trout aren't the only fishy thing around here." Mary snatched the promiscuous parcel from a counter, waved it furiously and scolded, "Go to your room." Gavin put the fish into an empty sink basin before he trudged upstairs.

F. Lee Bailey would've pled a Nolo Contendere defense. The convicted culprit trusted his transgression may be an inevitable capital offense. It was the worst violation he had ever committed.

Butch Reynolds parked in the garage. Mary unleashed a verbal tirade when her husband strode through the rear residence threshold. She ranted rabidly. The house filled with an irate dissonant diatribe and Gavin's disquietude dilated.

Mary chattered for ten minutes. The maddened mother beseeched, "I know you've never spanked Gavin but he needs discipline. We've already received Vice

Principal Wagner's depraved degenerate diagnosis."
Mary ushered her daughter outside as she explicated,
"Sara and I'll be at the grocery store."

Butch pondered the miniature ash wood oar shaped
punishment paddle on a granite fireplace mantel and
ambled upstairs without it. The gracious father opposed
flagellation. He reached Gavin's room, gently opened the
door and stated, "Hey Buddy." Gavin laid on the bed
while he bawled, "I'm sorry." Butch attempted to
alleviate the crestfallen child's distress. He sat in the desk
chair and promised, "Don't worry Gavin. I'm here so we
can chat."

An unorthodox milestone occurred. Butch kindly
counseled, "You're not old enough to read adult
publications but a bit of curiosity is normal. Your mother
and sister shouldn't see man magazines. That's why it
says 'Entertainment for Men.' Do you get my drift?"
Gavin wasn't certain he understood his father's
implication. The astounded youngster responded,"Yes
Sir." Butch assigned penance as he pronounced, "You'll
split and stack extra firewood until school begins next
week."

Gavin was speechless when his dad summarized the
merciful judgment with an astute observation. The
thoughtful elder said, "A beating isn't good for anyone.
Us playboys gotta stick together."

Today an antique hangs on Gavin's kitchen wall.
Mary gifted the swatter over three decades ago. Gavin

heeded Butch's advice so he didn't use injurious implements. The flogging foe employed exercise's curative effects during his son and daughter's terrible twos. When the siblings misbehaved they jogged laps around their one acre yard. The progenies earned first grade Presidential Physical Fitness Award patches.

Butch Reynolds died at the age of 78. A few months thereafter Gavin remembered his dad when he saw several cumulus clusters. The sight inspired imaginings about Butch's eternity. Gavin hoped his father's spirit inhabited the heaven he deserved. Perhaps it was an idyllic paradise where the softhearted soul made merry with dearly departed friends and family while they watched celestial angel Playmates cavort on cotton candy clouds. This version of Zion might be a distinct possibility. After all Hugh Hefner works in mysterious ways.

Montana Misfits

Friendships are frequently forged because of hardship. When individuals experience a strenuous situation and strive together they learn reliance. Calamitous circumstances challenged three Robert Long Pool Summer Swim Camp survivors. Gavin, Mike and Danny helped each other pass the cruel course. Their shared struggle catalyzed an alliance that grew as time went on. The pals founded a renegade bicycle club after third grade. Multiple vacation adventures transformed the boisterous buddies into an exclusive squad. The Ravalli County Rebels rampaged raucously.

When Gavin, Danny and Mike started their fourth year of academic incarceration a new boy attended classes. Charlie Harper came from Wenatchee, Washington. His family rented an abode near Gavin Reynolds' residence before the autumn semester commenced. The two young neighbors instantly bickered and refused a respectful relationship. An involuntary sleepover concluded violently. Gavin was sent home with a black eye due to an intense comic book controversy. The antagonists then quarreled about Elvis Presley and Johnny Cash a week later. Bloody noses terminated the altercation abruptly.

The spiteful stranger sported an atypical Pompadour hairstyle. Charlie hadn't visited Hamilton's tonsorial terror. The merciless coiffeur provided limited options. Danny, Mike and Gavin opted for crew cuts or flat tops. Their mothers didn't allow the bald barber's monumental Mohawks. Patrons feared the sociopath's trimmers. They sat still while the sadistic snipper menaced with electric clipper torture devices and razor sharp scissors. When customers complained the nutcase usually rubbed his shiny shaven head as he threatened, "If you don't like the way I buzz your scalp I can shear it shorter than mine." The inhumane haircut specialist's handiwork branded boy's ears. Lacerations and neck scars were standard. The ex-Marine earned his moniker. He was called Maniac Mick.

Charlie's clothes contrasted his contemporaries. Unlike the Chuck Taylor sneakers that locals wore he preferred Dingo Men's Dean Harness Boots. The nonconformist didn't try to fit in with blue jeans and t-shirt clad boys. Charlie favored flare leg corduroy pants. Polyester turtlenecks completed his aberrant attire.

It soon became evident Charlie was tough. He resembled a prison convict during his first recess at Jefferson Elementary School. The gutsy kid picked an unwinnable fight with a barbaric bully. Stan Morris mutilated Charlie. An enormous fat lip did earn the defeated fisticuff fellow a modicum of admiration from his confounded classmates.

Charlie's cussing capabilities were colossal. He stupendously shouted several spectacular word sequences subsequent to an inglorious dodge ball debacle. His dumbstruck audience hadn't previously perceived profanities proclaimed as proficiently. The outrageous orator's lewd language was renowned. When Charlie blurted a blasphemous bluster because of an inedible soggy sandwich Danny praised the creative curser's crude comment approvingly. The expletive extoller exclaimed, "I swear that scoundrel can really swear!" Even severe detractors relented. Mike discreetly admitted, "Everybody's gotta have at least a single pleasant personality peculiarity."

Gavin's mother devised an armistice and reconciliation plan three weeks after Charlie's arrival. Mary compelled her son to take the newcomer fishing. Gavin normally accompanied his chums on Saturday but the meddlesome matriarch nixed their participation. She was sure Charlie would be a better influence than Danny and Mike.

Mary persistently persuaded her peeved progeny prior to the piscatory pursuit. Gavin expressed opposition. He paced on the porch and propounded, "Charlie probably detests fishing." Mary rebutted her unhappy offspring. The stringent female ordered, "Stop whining. You're taking Charlie. Fetch him and tell his mother thank you. Polite is always right." Gavin lost the argument decisively. The sullen sourpuss squawked, "Sufferin' succotash." Mary finished the fusser's defiance. She shook her left index finger and commanded, "Do as I say. Come back for your lunches Sweetie."

Gavin returned with Charlie. Both malcontents bypassed Mrs. Reynolds and went into the garage. Gavin glimpsed at the greenhorn as he mocked, "What kind of an ignoramus doesn't own a fishing rod?" Charlie stood in an aggressive Rockem Sockem Robot stance. The grouchy guest grumbled, "A thug like me." Gavin shrugged smugly, handed Charlie an awry fishing pole and portrayed a benevolent benefactor. The pretend patron proposed, "You can use this one. It's my favorite." The battered Berkley spinning rod's tip was bent and two eyelets were misshapen. Gavin predicted the damaged fishing pole made it impossible for Charlie to catch anything.

Future failure was further assured. Gavin considerately supplied an inoperable Mitchell reel. The defective apparatus had been spooled with tangled 2-4lb test line. Gavin also dispensed a pocket sized tackle box. It contained three mangled lures, two barbless rusty hooks and an indented bobber. The clever saboteur's scheme finalized when he gave Charlie a fetid fish creel. Gavin presented the rancid pouch and cagily clarified, "Strong scents attract trout."

Perhaps the hoodwinker overembellished his prank. Gavin was ruffled when the ruse unraveled. Charlie unexpectedly threw the inferior equipment down as he snarled, "Fishing with you sucks!"

Gavin's angry adversary espied an immaculate Daisy Model 25 that hung above the workbench. Charlie slinked forward, snatched the BB caliber rifle and sneered, "This boom boom stick's bodacious." The callous interloper who defied firearms decorum enraged Gavin. He indignantly demanded, "Give me my gun right now! Morons play with weapons."

Charlie reluctantly consented. He relinquished the rifle and utilized a universal aphorism. Nobody aspires to look like an ignoble coward. The coercer clucked and cackled, "Are you yellow? Let's take that peashooter with us."

Influential intimidation prevailed. Gavin eschewed a spineless pansy assessment. The practical posturer acquiesced and conceded, "We could bring my gun for protection. Lots of grizzlies live by the river." Gavin hoped an exaggeration would make the pesky pariah quit, tuck tail and flee. He was disappointed when Charlie responded, "Cool. I've always wanted to bag a bear."

Gavin understood he needed permission. The realist wisely obeyed one of his father's cardinal criterions. He set the weapon aside and specified, "Let's get our lunches. I'll ask to use the BB gun. We'll grab my wrist rocket. Sidearms are sometimes necessary."

Butch Reynolds sat at an oak kitchen table when both boys burst through the back doorway. Gavin breathlessly beseeched, "Dad can we take the BB gun?" Butch didn't answer immediately. The arbiter chewed his fried baloney sandwich morsel slowly. He skeptically eyeballed the anxious whippersnappers and seriously sanctioned, "It's alright but you guys must behave responsibly. If I hear about any hijinks there will be consequences."

The scamps reacted promptly. Gavin retrieved the slingshot and procured field rations. He sped to the garage with Charlie. The self starter snappily stuffed lunch sacks, fishing paraphernalia, a Daisy 350-Count cardboard ammo container and his wrist rocket in an Army rucksack. Ergonomics were engendered efficiently. Gavin put his carryall on, picked up a spinning rod and the BB gun.

Posthaste performance was initiated by Charlie. He packed pathetic excuses for angling gear into the putrid canvas creel. Charlie draped it around his shoulder and grasped the loaned fishing pole. Within an instant the synchronized associates embarked on their excursion. Gavin marched like a soldier and Charlie kept in step. Wagner's "Ride of the Valkyries" suited an improbable occasion.

Gavin and Charlie approximated tramps as they trekked towards the Bitterroot River resolutely. The wayfarers passed a National Guard Armory decommissioned tank when Charlie remarked, "Now I see why you begged to borrow the BB gun. Your old man seems stern." Charlie's diplomatic observation surprised Gavin. The uncertain kid nodded and replied, "My dad has strict rules but he's not so bad."

It was an uncomfortably humid morning. The schoolmates slogged sulkily. Gavin panted and protested, "I wish we had bikes." Charlie spouted similar opinions. The miserable hiker moaned, "I destroyed a Sears Spyder during an unregulated Wenatchee dirt track race. My folks shopped for a replacement but no hicksville stores sell decent demo models. Pops has an appointment in Missoula today. He promised to buy a new Schwinn bicycle."

Charlie and Gavin arrived at an unoccupied beach beside the Main Street Bridge. They rested alongside a large flat boulder. Gavin tossed his pack on the rock and suggested, "I'm hungry. Time for lunch." The voracious chowhounds enjoyed an abundant tuna fish sandwich, barbecued chips, Ding Dongs and RC Cola feast. Charlie was unaccustomed to luxury so he complimented, "Your mom cooks a scrumptious picnic." Gavin devoured an ample Hostess dessert bite and solemnly warned Charlie. The tipster emphatically exhorted, "Don't let her fine food fool you. She can be ruthless as a rattlesnake."

Gavin decided he shouldn't show Charlie his confidential fishing spots. The pragmatist also didn't want to angle in overfished waters near town. Gavin held the BB gun like an exemplary cadet and submitted, "How's about a hunt. There's wooded land across the river. We'll walk over the bridge and rustle up blue grouse flocks."

Charlie concurred eagerly. He slurped soda pop and croaked, "Awesome." The brilliant baritone sustained his splendid intonation. Gavin was astonished by the tremolo crooner's ability to burp and speak simultaneously. Charlie's ingenious vocal feat flabbergasted the fascinated spectator. Gavin soon saluted the silver tongued wordsmith's supreme linguistic aptitude. Charlie had shortcomings but his impolite pronouncements were unparalleled.

Gavin applauded the talented toad impersonator and cheered, "Your belches are world class. Encore!" Charlie was accustomed to requests. The effervescent emoter chugged carbonated cola before he flouted a fervid emulation of an American bullfrog. Charlie bulged out his eyes and gulped deeply as if he had ingested a fly. The eloquent exhaler burped loudly while he bellowed, "Let's go!"

Unsupervised rambunctious rascals relished the Riverview Cemetery's lack of authority figures. Inert inhabitants left rabble-rousers alone. Gavin's perilous encounters with the grumpy groundskeeper were an exception. The thick accented German immigrant's full name was Gustav Von Quatschkopf. His carefree kid abhorrence exceeded the *Chitty Chitty Bang Bang* Child Catcher's animosity.

When Gavin and Charlie approached the entrance they didn't see Gustav's green Chevy step side pickup truck. Anonymous intrusion was implemented as Gavin ardently urged, "The crackpot coot's gone. Follow me." The zealous boys zigzagged through tombstones. Both scurriers then entered a forest behind the remembrance garden. No living souls witnessed the intrepid trespassers.

Gavin and Charlie trotted until they came upon an immense cedar stump. Sweat seeped substantially. Gavin leaned the BB gun and fishing rod against tree trunk remnants painstakingly. The escort took off his backpack while he whispered, "This is base camp. Keep your voice low so we can hear dangerous wildlife like a berserk bull moose that trapped my dad in an elm tree for a whole day."

Charlie was averse to arduous marches. The blister sufferer sat on an inclined log and removed his right boot. He realized Gavin might sense ineptitude. The fibber fabricated falsehood when he carped, "These Dingoes weren't broken in." Gavin peered at the poorly shod griper and razzed, "Is Montana too rough for Washington weaklings? Every dope knows Chuck Taylors are the ultimate wilderness shoe." Charlie's painful footwear resolve evolved. The egotist swallowed vanity and purchased Converse All Stars from Bob Ward's Sports & Outdoors store a few weeks later.

Gavin was heedless of his bombasity when he introduced an ostentatious hunter safety course. The ranter unwittingly aped Barney Fife as he dramatically disclosed, "I'll explain firearms procedures." Gavin picked up the rifle purposefully. The pompous pontificator aimed at a ponderosa pine and pestered, "Listen up. Weapon awareness is paramount. There's an incalculable difference between this Daisy Model 25 and a regular BB gun. It's like comparing an infantry bazooka to a cork pistol."

Charlie became interested in the supercilious sermonizer's subject. He interrupted his tactless tutor's pretentious monologue. The swollen heel soother questioned, "How does it work?" Gavin grimaced, gripped the wooden stock and instructed, "This is an incremental pump action armament. Each air injection generates higher firepower. I personally recommend five pumps. Any more disintegrates the target. Always keep the safety on until you shoot. A gazillion klutzes lost their toes because they fiddled with loaded BB guns."

The lecture lengthened. Gavin simulated an assiduous drill sergeant. He cleared his throat and expounded, "I'll load the gun to demonstrate how it's done. Remove the shot tube. Squish the spring then pour BBs into this hole. Release the coil gently. Last of all reinsert the gadget. My rifle reloads automatically so a sniper can repeat rounds rapidly. Many European countries outlaw the weapon."

Gavin ended his haughty seminar as he queried, "Have you ever been hunting?" Charlie put his boot back on and acted an amateur's role. The conniver claimed, "I fired my cousin's cap gun once." Gavin was unimpressed by the tyro's resume. He judgmentally scoffed, "You're a rookie. I'll take the first shot."

Both prigs pridefully perpetuated their provocation plans. Charlie resented Gavin's arrogant attitude and chose to serve his snooty companion an unappealing taste of humble pie. The habitual hoaxster was a practiced possum player. He craftily hornswoggled the Bitterroot blowhard.

Charlie's repugnance was reciprocated. Gavin begrudged the critic's constant contempt. He loathed the nasty tempered neophyte who maligned Montana. Gavin craved the snotty brat's abasement. He intended to discredit the devilish disputant.

Gavin shouldered his rifle and placed the extra ammunition into an empty pants pocket. The denigrator dictated a disdainful directive as he declared, "Hunting's like war. Keep your mouth shut and eyes open. Stay behind me so you don't get bisected by BB gun blasts."

The condescension irritated Charlie. He rancorously requested, "Whatever dude. When do I shoot?" Gavin glared at the bellicose squabbler and made his displeasure obvious. The ungracious guide gruffly growled, "You'll get an equal chance hotshot. Grab the fish creel. We'll use it as a bird bag."

Gavin and Charlie crept via an almost invisible trail. The pugnacious pair heard a grouse covey. Gavin stopped and held his left hand up while he stated, "There are birds in the brush. Be quiet so I can draw them out." The skillful stalker focused. He pumped the rifle five times. Gavin cooed "tu, tu, tu" noises. It was an incredible imitation of the animal's continuous yodel. A medium sized hen wobbled from an aspen tree's undergrowth. Gavin deactivated the safety, raised his BB gun and squeezed off a round.

An infinitesimal dust cloud suddenly exploded. Gavin's quarry hooted hysterically as it sprang skyward and flew away. The panic stricken critter was uninjured. Gavin swore softly. The harried hunter hissed, "Son of a biscuit!" He clicked the safety on and rationalized, "These sights must be crooked. I had that prairie chicken dead to rights."

Charlie celebrated Gavin's misfortune. The ornery opportunist clapped and chuckled as he heckled, "Nice job ace." Gavin did the honorable thing hesitantly. The flop forked over his BB gun. Charlie scrutinized the rifle briefly and determinedly decreed, "Cover my six." Charlie's exact edict stunned Gavin. The befuddled boy suspiciously mused, "Why does an imbecile seem so confident?"

Weapons were Harper family tradition but Charlie still shrouded his sharpshooter status. The marksman who posed as a novice had dispatched dozens of birds. He was well acquainted with the twenty gauge Remington 870 Fieldmaster an elder lent him while they sought ring-necked pheasants and chukar partridges. Charlie also didn't inform Gavin about a Winchester Model 70 he shot to drop an eight point mule deer. The fraudster fathomed firearms and hunting protocol prodigiously.

Both rivals traveled until they detected disturbances in a distant cottonwood. An unidentifiable fowl fluttered. The intrigued nimrods instinctively crouched. Charlie pumped the stock seven times. He disabled the safety, aimed and asserted, "I can plug it from here." Gavin assumed the boastful boy had exaggerated. The cynic contended, "I'll bet a quarter you'll miss."

Gavin was shocked when the supposedly untrained gunslinger stood like an adept duck hunter and zeroed in on his prey. Charlie exhaled as he pulled the trigger adroitly. The tiny bird tumbled. Charlie smiled with satisfaction and engaged the safety expertly. The deadeye death dealer giggled giddily while he gloated, "This thing shoots swell."

The contrarians cantered to a contorted corpse. Charlie crowed, "You owe me twenty five cents!" Gavin's dexterous deportment discombobulated. He gaped at the creatures mottled brown wings speechlessly.

The avian had an iridescent yellow throat with a black v-shape. Gavin distinguished the bird's species. Nausea inundated him. He puked an eruption of tuna fish, Wonder Bread, barbecued potato chips, a Ding Dong and RC Cola profusely. The vigorous vomiter spat bile before he yelled, "You're an idiot!"

Charlie derided his host's herculean regurgitation. The ridiculer taunted, "I guess Bitterroot yokels can't stomach slaughter." Gavin garnered the mishaps magnitude so he bitterly barked, "You shot a meadowlark. It's Montana's State Bird. When the Department of Fish and Wildlife catches us we're going to jail"

Agitation ensued as Charlie sobered quickly. He evaluated his error and enunciated an explicit vile vernacular barrage. The blunderer vented vexation until he urgently uttered, "Let's scram." Charlie had been on the lam and construed it was crucial to disguise their tracks. He seized control of the site like a Gambino family fixer. Charlie toed the feathered fatality frustratedly. The shrewd sidestepper insisted, "That stupid bird's gotta disappear. We shouldn't bury the body here. Investigators might use bloodhounds. Those mangy sniffer mutts would definitely smell the carcass. You go back with the rifle while I clean this mess."

Charlie secreted his assassination victim in the odoriferous creel and swept plumage away with an alder bush branch. The caper concealer descried a crimson colored dirt clot. Charlie scuffed the soil intently. An incriminating stain dissipated. He fastidiously examined the scene. No trace evidence remained. The forensic fragment eliminator rejoined his queasy colleague.

Gavin and Charlie reclaimed their gear before they hurried to the necropolis border in tandem. The attentive absconders viewed a virtually vacant vicinity. Gus's vehicle was parked by the maintenance building's open door. Regretfully the retreaters maneuvers required reconsideration.

The Bitterroot River and patrolled private property blocked substitute escape routes. Gavin deduced the burial ground was their sole evacuation recourse. He surveyed an inactive vista and implored, "That crusty kook's inside the shed. Race you to the gate."

Charlie and Gavin had sprinted halfway through a headstone horde when the belligerent Bavarian emerged. Gustav wielded an edging shovel. The mean spirited man from Munich mirrored a *Scooby-Doo, Where Are You!* mystery villain. He swung the spade savagely and screamed, "You darn delinquents better leave my boneyard!" The tempestuous Teutonic chased for ten yards. Gustav smoked cigarettes insatiably so he gasped greatly and halted. The spoilsport Saxon resoundingly rasped, "Run hooligans otherwise I'll entomb both of your buttocks!"

Gavin and Charlie exited an eternal rest acreage egress. The fugitives traipsed towards town. When they crossed the Main Street Bridge Gavin mentioned a potent problem. He prudently posited, "What about the dang meadowlark?"

The abettors reached an east side river embankment. Charlie handed the flawed fishing pole to Gavin. The roguish James Cagney movie fan knew criminal cadaver disposal etiquette. Charlie snickered like his gangster film hero and inserted a cantaloupe sized rock into the creel competently. The mobster mimicker smirked while he reassured, "We don't have concrete boots but this stone should work nicely. I'll make the bird vanish."

No one else was at the location. Charlie and Gavin scrambled to an oval shaped shoreline boulder under the bridge. They climbed onto the massive granite overhang agilely. The culprits couldn't be seen from above. Charlie hurled the creel into a swift current. It made an indistinct "gloop" sound and submerged. The bird butcher reckoned he had committed a perfect crime. Charlie brashly bragged, "Let's see those dirty rat game wardens nab us now."

The artful accomplices ambled into Hamilton. Past precarious predicaments enlightened Charlie. He appreciated the advantages of an alibi. The remorseless ruffian conveyed his wisdom when he advised, "If anybody asks we'll say I shot a starling. Believable lies are always closest to the truth."

Gavin had prevaricated sporadically and comprehended an effective fictitious explanation was rare. The astute equivocator validated Charlie's valuable acumen as he argued, "Nobody likes starlings. Everyone hunts them. My Aunt Ruby pays a Nickel bounty."

When the colluders strolled in front of Mr. Gelato's market Charlie inquired, "Where's the money?" Gavin attempted to evade his gambling debt. The financial obligation avoider advanced an alternative. He smoothly reasoned, "Keep the fishing pole. We'll repair it. I'll donate a reel and nicer creel that isn't so stinky."

Charlie grinned gladly. He finally had an authentic pal. The hellion from Wenatchee laughed and said, "Are all Montanans mutton headed misfits? I accept your offer but you still owe me two bits."

The unconventional comrades successfully snuck back into Gavin's garage. Happy hurrah hoopla heralded harmony. Conspiracy created confidants. Attitudes adapted and mutual mistrust mutated miraculously. It's funny how a boy's worst enemy can become his best friend.

Decades passed and Gavin gave up guns long ago. The grandfather recalled an important insight he acquired during youth. Hunting taught him about life's fragility. Gavin was like most children who lived in rural America. He respected weapons and recognized their lethality. The Ravalli County rapscallion ascertained a fundamental fact at an early age. When something's dead there are no second chances. Gavin shot a deer on his fourteenth birthday. He discerned the deceased doe's glassy eyes and never discharged firearms again.

An implacable conscience bothered Gavin after the western meadowlark killing. He rued his actions forty eight years later. The contrite curmudgeon carried culpability compunctiously. Gavin's mistake might seem minor but a valuable lesson was learned. An impulsive incident can instigate unrectifiable repercussions. Fortunately the Bitterroot boys only slayed a songbird.

The Cub Scout Caper

The Ravalli County Rebels were a legendary renegade bicycle gang in Hamilton, Montana. Their mischievous mayhem missions started scads of Bitterroot Valley scandals. Fourth grade began for the fraternal order's three members. Mike, Danny and Gavin didn't readily accept crew candidates.

When Charlie Harper first attended Jefferson Elementary School the biker club treated him as an enemy. Gavin effectuated a conversion of opinion. He had hunted blue grouse with Charlie and an improbable detente emerged due to a dire debacle. The tyke's tenacity transformed Gavin's prejudice. An accidental western meadowlark assassination aftermath catalyzed cordiality. Charlie's companionless circumstance ceased.

Subsequent to the state bird slaying Gavin recounted a revised report. The embellisher notified his clubmates at an iron school bike rack before classes began. Danny and Mike listened while the anecdotalist urged, "You nincompoops think he's a jerk but Charlie blasted that starling from fifty yards. The guy's an incredible sniper. He cusses and fist fights. We can use a scrapper with superior sabotage skills."

Danny also abandoned animosity. He accordingly assented, "Maybe Gavin's right. An unhinged psychopath who punched a bully like Stan Morris seems worthy."

Mike was uncertain if the quarrelsome kid could be trusted. The skeptic disputed, "Charlie's an annoying liar. He keeps making up excuses about why his father hasn't purchased a bike."

The school bell rang at 8am. Danny, Gavin and Mike saw Charlie as he pedaled an irradiant new bicycle. The confident cyclist cruised a coveted tricked out two wheeler. Charlie rode an opaque red and silver chrome sissy barred Schwinn Stingray. He likened a David Mann painting in *Easyriders* magazine. Charlie hastened across an unblemished patch of concrete sidewalk and skidded. His rear slicker tire imprinted a six foot long arched tread mark.

Gavin and his friends had prematurely postulated Charlie's BMX brags were boasts. The valorous venturer verified virtuosity. Contrary convictions changed after Mike conceded, "Charlie can join our club if he doesn't swear around my parents."

The Ravalli County Rebels ran towards Charlie. Danny shouted, "Primo!" and Gavin yelled, "Sweet bike!" Mike disguised an inkling of overt enthusiasm. He brandished a comb and slicked back his greasy flat top haircut. Mike peered at Charlie as he proffered, "Whoa. Whaddya say? Wanna be in our gang? We normally jump recruits into the club but your credentials are legit. I guess we'll make an exception."

Charlie smirked and enjoyed his prestige. He garnered the gullible gang hadn't encountered a capable culprit such as himself. The scallywag snickered, sneered and snarled, "Okie dokie. I ain't got nothing better to do in this Podunk town."

The rambunctious quartet stuck together throughout their fourth grade year. Ravalli County Rebel raids waned when winter weather materialized. The ruffians weren't permitted to rampage on icy streets. Danny, Charlie and Gavin lost interest in the club. An unloyal secessionist movement gained traction. Three ungrateful chums considered Cub Scouts of America enlistment.

Mike was ticked off with his traitorous buddies. He eyeballed the betrayers and berated, "You bums are a bunch of finks. Go ahead. Become stupid scout sellouts. See if I care."

Danny advocated the allegiance amendment when he responded, "Come on Mike. It's December and indoor Ravalli County Rebel stuff is boring."

Gavin supported his mutinous abettor. The empiricist added, "Archery training and tomahawks are available." Defectors formed an irrefutable majority as Charlie mentioned, "Noose knots sound useful."

Mike was remarkably realistic. He recanted and related, "Okay. I'll join until we restart our biker gang next spring. By then you dunces will find out what I know. Goodie gumdrop Cub Scouts suck."

A few days after the pals agreed on an interim club sabbatical they attended their inaugural Cub Scout meeting at Jefferson Elementary School. The rogues raised right hands and recited a solemn oath. An austere code of conduct confounded the unaccustomed inductees. Dereliction developed directly. Danny, Mike, Charlie and Gavin deliberately defied draconian directives.

The malcontents deeply detested Cub Scout hierarchy. They profoundly deplored the Hamilton troop's tyrant. A den mother named Mrs. Scott topped the chapter's chain of command. Her similarities to Joseph Stalin were innumerable. The malicious matron's deputy was an amenable sycophant who served as den leader. Mrs. Scott's son Kevin held the position for three consecutive months. He inflicted pernicious edicts remorselessly.

Mrs. Scott's policies decreed a boy became temporary den leader upon his birthday. Discrepant terms ended when another scout's natal date arrived. Gavin complained about disparate durations and Mrs. Scott disdainfully divulged, "I don't write the rules young man. I just enforce them."

Gavin purported propriety was possible. He devised an equitable remedy. The entry level rank Bobcat suggested a regulation realignment. One fateful afternoon Gavin respectfully lifted his left hand until Mrs. Scott impatiently sighed, "What's your quibble?"

The insubordinate inciter recklessly recommended, "Wouldn't it be better if we rotated den leader monthly. That way everybody gets an equal chance."

Mrs. Scott manifested malevolence without a word. The wrathful woman grimaced and harrumphed emphatically. Her contorted face was crimson. Mrs. Scott stomped several steps, grabbed Gavin's elbow and herded him into the hall hastily. The huffy harridan commenced condemnation. She angrily castigated, "Why do you and your little friends disrupt my agenda? Your mother will soon hear about the headaches you hellions instigate."

Gavin discerned what Grandpa Joe Reynolds meant when the patriarch advised, "Life isn't fair." The reprimanded boy returned to an unoccupied chair and sat quietly. He sourly stared at Downing Mountain. Gavin's mute mopy manner was worrisome.

Mrs. Scott wheeled a large cardboard container atop an appropriated custodian's cart into the classroom. She opened the conundrum's lid and took out a package. The duplicitous den mother disclosed, "These are Pinewood Derby car kits. We aren't building models and won't be competing in the Stevensville race. I cannot chaperone because of my family's reunion. Pick up your boxes while you leave. I'm not an unpaid storage facility. Meeting adjourned."

Gavin scowled and snatched a parcel from the cart as he silently stormed away. His pals strolled with him across an idyllic snowy schoolyard. Gavin stewed irately until Danny queried, "What did Mrs. Scott say?" Gavin unleashed rage. He hurled the Pinewood Derby car kit skyward and spouted, "She's gonna contact my mother. Mrs. Scott's out to annihilate us."

Mike seized the dismal moment. He gleefully gloated, "The Ravalli County Rebels don't seem bad now. Unlike Mrs. Scott I am a principled leader. I'd never snitch to your mothers. Even if you were dead."

Charlie's negative evaluation was comparable. He reviled the den mother's repressive regimentation and remonstrated, "She constantly reminds me to wear an imbecilic scarf that mimics General Custer."

Danny appended the stupendous smear campaign. He one upped prior pique. The concurrent critic confided, "Her Rice Crispy treats gave me diarrhea." Danny's dangerous dyspepsia diagnosis disheartened the defamers. They realized their den mother was a cereal killer.

The extraordinary envenomed episode exacerbated enmity. Mike recognized lives were imperiled. He fervently fulminated, "Let's meet at my house tomorrow after school. We'll figure out how to eradicate the fiend before she slays us." The irresolute insurrectionists immediately endorsed revolution.

Charlie, Danny and Gavin attended Mike's emergency confab. Their host's domicile was parentless until dinnertime. The resistance ringleader sat at his kitchen table and chewed an Oreo cookie as he soliloquized strategy. Mike's initial conjecture clarified a coup. The maleficent mastermind extolled, "We need to run Mrs. Scott out of office. It's her or us. Maybe an ethical mom will take over."

The other boy's were hesitant about Mike's mania. Danny reanalyzed ramifications. The vacillator jabbered, "I've never gotten sick from her Jell-O squares."

Mike contradicted Danny's apprehensive articulation. He pounded his fist on the tabletop and growled, "You lily livered losers want to wimp out like a bunch of weenies!"

Gavin sustained an incompatible viewpoint. Punitive den mother phone recriminations generated extra chores. Plentiful past tribulations because of Mike's brazen brainstorms also influenced his reluctance. Gavin prognosticated an inept uprising would be lamentable. The wary pragmatist expounded, "Mrs. Scott's a crafty customer. She breeds bees in her bonnet."

Mike glared gruffly. He leapt from an oak stool, lividly loped across a linoleum floor and apprised, "That Hades hound is an inhumane hornet's nest. It's our duty as American citizens to end her fascism. You nervous nellies live in a democracy!"

Charlie was intimidated by the merciless matriarch. He hadn't opposed the magnitude of depravity Mrs. Scott disbursed. The downtrodden scamp shook his noggin dourly and declared, "AWOL's the smart thing to do."

Mike became enraged. His friends were emasculated entirely. The asperser contemptuously mocked, "You cowardly crybabies could've joined the Girl Scouts!" He then cantankerously chastised, "You spineless scaredy-cats enable the Jezebel's belittlement! Have you forgotten Evel Knievel's advice? Nothing is impossible. We can crush the Delilah!" Mike respired robustly and resurrected his rant. The reproacher emulated an evangelist while he adamantly asserted, "Mrs. Scott choreographs a Cub Scout den of iniquity. How many times do we allow the harlot's treachery? Even Adam wasn't dumb enough to eat an orange Eve offered him after the apple."

A hush ensued until Mike revealed his plot to dethrone the diabolical den mother dramatically. The conscientious crusader detailed countermeasures when he implored, "That sister of Satan nixed our Pinewood Derby activities. Regional scout masters will be at the races. We'll tell them about the Lucifer lady and they'll fire her. I don't care what the devil's daughter decided. I'm entering Stevensville's championship! Who's with me!"

Mike should've been the scion of Pentecostal preacher. His dad was an introverted and extremely pious Catholic. Nevertheless Mike's homily saved three subdued souls. The browbeaten buddies were converted. Mike's sermon reformed the disconcerted comrades' misguided ways.

Tomes could be written regarding Pinewood Derby bylaws but the paramount requirement was that a boy's miniature vehicle weighed less than five ounces. Heavy cars were generally faster. An aerodynamic design and lubricated wheels also increased velocity.

Brilliant boys assembled their kits sans supervision. Absent EPA, Child Protective Services and OSHA administrators affirmed the wisdom of government deregulation. Bureaucrat buttinskies bypassed the laissez-faire undertaking. Hazards such as lead exposure and vapor poisoning were unheralded during the kinder gentler era.

Perseverance was the crucial character trait to actualize a Pinewood Derby car. Hopeful boys deployed dull pocket knives when they sculpted seven inch wood blocks. The whittlers gouged galena receptacle cavities. Finicky scouts sanded the object's surface. Splinter removal tweezers were invaluable.

An awkward step came next. Four evenly spaced axle recepticles were augered. It was virtually unfeasible to accomplish the procedure without a jig, drill press or an intact 3/32 bit. Scouts typically didn't possess proper equipment. Innovative boys used handheld borers and siblings as vices.

FBI bomb disposal experts executed easier assignments than tinkerers who installed Pinewood Derby car axles and wheels. Delicate dexterous protocol approximated brain surgery. If the tires aligned correctly it was a miracle. The fragile parts commonly bent. Shaky hands rendered broken mechanisms useless. Sales of replacement components surpassed three hundred thousand dollars annually.

An abundance of puncture wounds proliferated. Lucidious lawyers prospered as impaled youngsters' legal counsel. A bazillion bloodied and befuddled boys desisted because of axle anxiety. The agonizing defeat curtailed countless Cub Scout careers.

Nearly all toymakers decorated the car's wood body. Some painters preferred monochromatic speedsters while others favored pinstriped roadster motifs. Fume intoxicated imps daubed highly flammable Testors Gloss Enamel in unventilated clandestine cubbyholes. Gregarious giggles gushed and hallucinatory hysteria heightened. Inebriates strived by candlelight into the wee night hours. Lightheaded laborers perfected colorant applications and an effulgent shellac varnish was then applied. Lastly brushes were cleaned in a mineral spirits filled vessel.

At this point Pinewood Derby cars usually weighed around four ounces. Cerebral boys scrutinized heftiness on grocery produce section scales. The mathematicians calculated how much lead they would affix. Sagacious scouts utilized an unauthorized hot plate and a cooking pot as an electric induction forge. Fledgling foundrymen poured 621.5 degree liquid inside of their car's compartment. Manifold metallurgists muffed the maneuver with bare knuckles and ended up in burn care units. Scald survivors prudently procured leather gloves after epidermis injuries maimed meathooks.

Industrious race car builders reweighed their creations. Many scouts shaved either wood or lead until the model vehicle satisfied specifications. The arduous endeavor culminated. Intrepid boys who navigated the right of passage without lifelong scars, neurosis or penniless piggy banks earned a significant victory.

Mike, Gavin, Danny and Charlie prioritized secrecy when they built Pinewood Derby cars. The astute artisans avoided adult assistance. Danny's dad worked swing shift so the resourceful dissidents toiled in his family's garage. Each boy manufactured an opus. Even Mike made a minimalist masterpiece.

Group ambitions were hampered by two hurdles. Firstly misinformation had to be mobilized. The pals lacked an alibi that described their whereabouts while they visited Stevensville. Another obstacle Gavin, Mike, Charlie and Danny faced was covert transportation.

Charlie solved the rideshare riddle. He competently compelled, "We need someone who can fib a cover story and drive us to the Derby discreetly. The only guy cool enough is Gavin's Uncle Steve."

Gavin suspected Charlie's convenient panacea. The dissenter intuited deception. He heatedly howled, "Doggone it! What's Uncle Steve supposed to tell our moms and dads?"

Mike appeased the distressed dupe diligently. The availer averred, "Your uncle should say he has tickets for an upcoming basketball game. University of Montana plays Boise State the same afternoon as our race. He's lied previously. My parents reckon Uncle Steve's a Buddhist."

Gavin was contemptuous of the cabal's conspiracy. He gritted his teeth and barked, "Tarnation! You galoots are out to get me in trouble!"

Danny tipped the debate scales decisively. The coaxer contended, "Uncle Steve will do it. He despises disciplinarians like Mrs. Scott. I bet he'll appreciate Pinewood Derby races because of his jacked-up jalopy."

Gavin was outnumbered and outwitted. He presumed the dialogue had been orchestrated. The wordage seemed contrived. Gavin carried the onus nonetheless and heroically petitioned his elder's patronage.

Uncle Steve bartended at the bowling alley when Gavin requested reinforcement. The vehement Vietnam veteran comprehended justice superseded statutory trivialities. He had experienced altercations with mud slingers. Uncle Steve mixed Gavin an on the house Roy Rogers and opined keen insight as he submitted, "We won't let that despot den mother win the war of wits. I'll chauffeur and tell your folks about the basketball game. Sometimes a dude's gotta mislead oppressors to maintain integrity."

Races transpired the following Saturday. Uncle Steve met Danny, Charlie, Gavin and Mike at Mr. Gelato's market. Each boy toted an inconspicuous shoebox. The scouts climbed into their collaborator's automobile. Uncle Steve observed, "I dig your uniforms. They're similar to the service dress blues I wore home from Nam." The charitable driver turned a brass ignition key and his vehicle roared. He elevated the eight track cassette player's volume. Creedence Clearwater Revival's hit "Suzie Q" blared through custom speakers.

The insurgents motored beyond Daly Mansion and Gavin asked, "What kind of cigarette are you smoking? My dad's Pall Malls smell different." Uncle Steve mentored meticulously. The noncompliant iconoclast imparted, "It's particularly potent Panama tobacco."

Uncle Steve was an avid Richard Petty fan. He drove a Plymouth Road Runner with 7.0 Hemi V-8 engine. His orange and black spoiler muscle machine zoomed. Montana laws stipulated no speed limit. Uncle Steve exploited the loophole. He averaged seventy five miles per hour during the sixteen minute trip.

Four ordinarily loquacious boys were speechless and white knuckled when they arrived at Stevensville High School. Uncle Steve promised to pick up the contestants later before he accelerated away. Mike surveyed his surroundings and warned, "I was here for an AAU Wrestling Tournament. Some of these thugs are pretty tough. One dipstick dislocated my shoulder. Be on your toes." The cohorts entered gymnasium doors warily and approached a registration counter.

An inspection committee sanctioned the infiltrators' cars. A judge arranged their entries on the restricted access table. Charlie, Gavin, Mike and Danny obtained participation certificates as the Missoula scoutmaster inquired, "Where's Mrs. Scott?" Mike's paranoid psyche was ready. He portrayed the role of an innocent munchkin convincingly. The tremendous truth twister emoted, "Our den mother's personal affairs are more important than this Pinewood Derby race."

Over a hundred cars were showcased systematically. The allies appraised their competition until they ensconced on an uninhabited wall backed gym mat pile that mollified Mike's distrustful disposition. He set his shoebox aside and insisted, "Let's sit here so goons can't jump us." The basketball court was a busy boy beehive. Mike assessed risk and cautioned, "Polson Webelos are vicious." An announcement from a blow horn squawked, "Attention scouts. Stand for our National Anthem." Bing Crosby's version of "The Star Spangled Banner" thundered through two treble toned speakers.

When the treasonous tetrad fabricated their cars Mike chose an uncomplicated configuration. He shrewdly averted self mutilation. The crude craftsman circumvented a carved construction. Mike's only modifications to the kit's wood polyhedron was an indigo paint job with claret flames and uneven wheels. The maladroit model maker touted his bulky brainchild as he argued, "My massive monolith is monumental."

Mike's concoction created chaos during the first heat. His contraption sped strongly after the starter gate dropped and ricocheted repeatedly. The timber chunk careened clunkily. It zig zagged and smashed into the right barrier. Two tires disconnected as the behemoth ejected out of lane number one. Mike's prototype propelled across the race track precariously. The deadly demolisher destroyed a Victor boy's dune buggy homage and launched laterally. An astounded Arlee adolescent injested a dislodged tooth when the lumber lump almost decapitated him. Fire extinguishers or ambulances weren't needed.

An investigation was consummated and Mike's dismantled devastator was disqualified. Race routines resumed. Two pack 2962 scouts reached the finals. Charlie's wedge shaped sensation came in second and Danny's El Camino inspired car placed fourth. Gavin's diminutive dragster finished seventh.

The triumphant Hamilton team received imitation bronze badges along with an engraved copper colored chalice. Medalists saluted the United States, Montana and Boy Scout flags while ceremonies concluded with a pimply tin eared teenager's acapella "God Bless America" rendition. The historic act of Pinewood Derby civil disobedience succeeded.

When the celebratory crew retrieved their cars Gavin exhorted, "We should give Uncle Steve our trophy." Unanimous ratification implemented instantly. Charlie and Danny slapped high fives. Mike caroused as he crowed, "My car's wipeout was awesome."

Uncle Steve's coupe idled in the principal's parking space. Charlie, Danny, Mike and Gavin got into the rumbling hotrod. Uncle Steve quelled the stereo decibels as he uttered, "How did it go?" Gavin handed his uncle the commendation cup excitedly and explained, "Keep the award because you helped us an awful lot." Uncle Steve gripped the statue and gulped. The recusant gratefully informed, "Thanks. I'll exhibit your prize at the bowling alley."

Gavin's uncle amplified the audio and peeled out. He sang along with subversive songs. His musical taste suited the aura aptly. The Road Runner rocketed via Corvallis as John Fogerty belted out "Fortunate Son." Uncle Steve warmly whooped, "Yahoo boys! Next stop is A & W. Your root beer floats are free!"

Three days passed until Charlie, Mike, Gavin and Danny pedaled their bikes to the next Cub Scout meeting. Four familiar station wagons sat beside Jefferson Elementary School ominously. The conquerors parked and crept through an entrance threshold. They were abruptly confronted by a female tribunal. Mrs. Scott led an inquisition. The prosecutorial den mother paced profusely. She pointed her left index finger furiously at the arraigned indictment recipients. Mrs. Scott mirrored Margret Hamilton's Wicked Witch of the West role marvelously. The scorner shrilly shrieked, "You miscreants ignored my mandate and raced in Stevensville."

A moral imperative motivated Mike. The asinine ad-libber believed he could prove Mrs. Scott was evil. Mike mistakenly assumed at least one witness would challenge the callous carper's cruelty, demand her resignation and commandeer control. The poorly prepared performer erred. He underestimated the power of an undeniable fact. No sane woman wants to be a den mother.

Mike valiantly validated. The bullheaded beginner barrister rashly replied, "Even though you welched on your responsibilities we raced and won third place." Aghast mothers gasped at Mike's obstinate cross examination. Gavin, Danny and Charlie fathomed their foolhardy friend's flounder. The trio futilely attempted to eschew culpability. Mike's somber sidekicks shuffled slowly. They separated from the audacious amateur attorney anxiously. Angst afflicted the accursed accomplices.

Mrs. Scott whirled towards the jury of ladies and loudly lambasted, "Do you hear these belligerent brat's insolence? Your unpatriotic pipsqueak boys are permanently expelled." The condemning croon furthered her vindictive verdict. She abashed an addled audience and affrontedly admonished, "Maybe you women should pay more attention to your children's unacceptable naughtiness." Mrs. Scott's castigation was complete. The pitiless persecutor marched away and slammed a classroom door shut.

Four mortified mothers assailed their seditious sons. Gavin's cranky caregiver hollered, "You better ride your bike home right now Mr. Smartipants!" Danny, Charlie and Mike's moms concurred with Mary Reynold's acerbity. They escorted the exiles outside vociferously. The maternal mob's simultaneous reprovals resembled rankled hens. Urgent escapes were necessary. The banished boys rapidly retreated.

Although sentences varied the ex-Cub Scouts each endured comeuppance. Gavin was grounded for two weeks and his loving mother demanded Catholic confession attendance. The uncontrite urchin skipped his avowal appointment. Father Edwards and Mrs. Reynolds benevolently bestowed an atonement regimen. The devout duo dutifully determined Ecclesiastical property landscaping tasks were a practical penance.

Charlie, Danny and Gavin boycotted Mike after they became Cub Scout persona non gratae. The shunned schoolmate addressed his ostracisers during lunch recess. Isolation confused him so he questioned, "What's your problem fellas?"

Danny's frustration fomented. The grump aggressively grumbled, "Why do we listen to you Mike? Your idiotic ideas cause catastrophes!" Gavin augmented

Danny's exasperation. The aggrieved church groundskeeper resented Mike's disastrous schemes and proclaimed, "I renounce the Ravalli County Rebels!" Charlie also testily terminated his bicycle brotherhood membership. The disparager defiantly deemed, "I quit Mike's lousy club!"

Mike pretended his feelings weren't hurt. The brave boy shrugged and speculated, "Maybe we can start an egalitarian gang. When you snivelers are in charge you'll learn it's not simple."

The three peeved pals relinquished their censorship. Mike's proposal was expedient. The confidantes sparked a substitute alliance. They discussed logistics throughout the mid day break. School bells clanged and Gavin diplomatically reasoned, "Leadership should be rotated so everyone screws up."

Mike laughed relievedly. He then tendered an obscure admission of wrongfulness. The pride swallower smiled and stated, "We all mess up occasionally." Mike's rationalization reactivated rapport. The four friends forgot their feud and forged forward.

Rebranding is a baffling subject for senior citizens. An obsessive trend to retitle engenders ambiguity. Tactful terminology has become taboo. A dodderer discovered different diction decorum five decades after his Cub Scout expulsion. Gavin was amidst an avocation when a regrettable incident occurred. The curious eccentric wandered around an immense home improvement center and stumbled upon a peculiar endcap display. Gavin found Pinewood Derby car kits that had recently been shipped from Shanghai, China.

It's hypothesized hindsight is twenty twenty. Gavin deduced the axiom might be untrue as he put on his $1.25 reading spectacles. The grumpy grandfather examined imported items and noticed an anomaly. Strangely the words Boy Scouts of America were absent. A promotional sign also omitted the organization. Gavin identified an apparent solution. It was something called the PSA.

A rhetorical retail representative approached Gavin and impolitely pronounced, "Yo boss. Did you find everything you're looking for?" The codger conjured composure and calmly quipped, "Does your establishment sell eternal enlightenment or inner peace?" Gavin's jocular jest galvanized an incredulous stare until the perceptive clerk posited, "You crazy old man!" The sarcastic geriatric ardently apologized, "I'm sorry. What happened to the Boy Scouts of America?"

Suddenly a bizarre situation worsened. The associate's anger erupted as he threatened, "Listen you gross geezer. Nobody speaks disrespectfully in our store. The offensive BSA slur is hurtful and politically incorrect. If I hear additional bigoted gender biased binary language I'll text security!"

Gavin was shocked by the reaction to his unintentional miscommunication. He alleged an inexplicable generation gap germinated the clerk's rabid rebuke. Gavin thought, "Has society gone insane?" The oldster contritely commented, "I'm inconversant with a lot of the newfangled acronyms. Please tell me what the letters PSA mean?"

The sophisticated hipster wielded an indispensable endorphin producer named Android fastidiously. His dependable digital device provided accurate world wide web answers. The customer service specialist swiftly swiped and announced, "PSA is a backronym. It means the People Scouts of America. Do you need anything else?" Gavin neglected to stop an irreverent mind that frequently fostered fracases as he said, "Which aisle are the lobotomy tools on?"

Swimming Hole Submarine

Marvel Comics' advertisements contained countless useful inventions. Stan Lee's publications were spectacular superhero sagas but several pages of an *Avengers* or *Amazing Spider-Man* featured newfangled novelties. Intrigued perusers purchased exotic oddities such as Sea Monkeys. Youngsters frugally saved allowances, paper route earnings and birthday cash to procure phenomenal innovations.

Most illustrated magazine marketers misrepresented merchandise. The surreptitious syndicate duped vulnerable readers whose fictional heroes epitomized ethics. Mail order miscreants preyed upon puzzled plebs who respected "Truth, Justice and the American Way." A paradox perplexed prepubescents. How could chivalrous cartoon champions coexist amongst fraudsters that hawked bunk?

Regardless of ruses moppet multitudes were unthwarted by hoaxes. They feverishly bought culinary pepper Magic Sneezing Powder. Subpar Seven Foot Monster posters and faulty X-Ray Specs constantly sold out. Keen kids invested in an ineffectual Money Making Machine to recoup their losses. Peeved printers discovered the cruddy currency was valueless.

Disreputable distributors who hyped wares in comic books promised, "10 Day Free Examination. Money back Guaranteed!" and "Zero Risk." The assurances were bogus. When dismayed customers wanted refunds return shipment of defective objects was required. The lengthy claim process inevitably voided warranties.

P.T. Barnum professed, "There's a sucker born every minute." The showman drastically underestimated. By 1965 it was proven an abundant amount of amiable numbskulls were birthed each nanosecond. Bitterroot Valley boys substantiated the accurate statistic. Ravalli County pawns paid umpteen dollars to comic book racketeers. After a gimmick premiered in an *Incredible Hulk* issue they gleaned the gizmo would surpass a Whoopie Cushion's wittiness.

Montana child welfare statutes were vague during the 1970's. Nevertheless when adults jettisoned juveniles off boats to sink or swim it wasn't condoned. Hamilton parents kept up with trends and avoided potential criminal indictment. They wisely enrolled their offspring in officially accredited American National Red Cross Swimming Lessons.

After Gavin Reynolds graduated from kindergarten he began two friendships at the Robert Long Memorial Pool's Summer Swimming School. Mike and Danny persevered with their new pal throughout an inhumane four week academy. The students commenced natation education in early June. Typically the 9am air temperature was around forty degrees.

The classmates ascertained they shared a common conclave of enemies known as Swimming School Staff after an introductory cold shower. Gavin initiated comradery when he observed, "Are all swim teachers insane?" Danny shivered and stuttered, "They're even meaner than nuns." Mike's teeth chattered. The purple faced boy babbled, "It's both. They're crazy and cruel."

Local parents didn't realize the high school aged lifeguard leaders were aquatic sociopaths. The callous cabal plied pitiless perilous persecution. Ignoble instructors utilized innocent terms such as Dandy Dolphin, Super Starfish, Awesome Otter and Golden Guppy to disguise their sadistic behavior. Joseph Goebbels couldn't have organized a more persuasive propaganda campaign.

If an internee complained about their captors they rapidly regretted a rash decision. Walrus Whistleblowers, Tadpole Traitors and Narwhal Narcs were punished promptly. Individuals deemed Seahorse Snitches or Unruly Urchins treaded water interminably. Descent wasn't tolerated. Austerity abided although alliteration advocacy abounded.

Mike, Gavin and Danny survived nineteen chilly mornings. The tenacious trio's twentieth day of tribulation transpired. They fidgeted atop frosty concrete and waited for permission to plunge in the pool. An intense rain storm pelted profusely. The hypothermic detainees convulsed as they tolerated teenage torturers' vicious verbal volleys.

Coach Cassandra emerged from the heated office, blew her whistle and yelled, "You Slimy Squids can stop your snivels. Deep end dives on the double!" Danny, Mike and Gavin jumped quickly. The frigid fluid was akin to a Slurpee. Mike surfaced and surmised, "This camp sucked but I guess it's better than an unexpected dunk in the river." Gavin bobbed beside the drain gutter and exclaimed, "My Grandpa Joe threw his children into Lake Como. When I gripe about these terrible tutors he laughs like a hyena." Danny's erudite empathy emanated. The scholarly savant sputtered, "Hundreds of Flathead County kids drown that way every year."

The contemptible course concluded. Mike, Gavin and Danny socialized subsequently. By the autumn semester's onset they were apt abettors. The confidantes' cooperation progressed. After third grade the accomplices founded an exclusive bicycle club. The Ravalli County Rebels shunned interlopers. Charlie Harper moved to Hamilton and shifted sentiments.

When the stranger first attended Jefferson Elementary School he wasn't welcomed magnanimously. The Ravalli County Rebels mocked Gavin's new neighbor relentlessly. They dubbed the outsider with a malicious moniker. After "Charlie Farter" came to town Gavin's mother forced fishing trip fraternization. Rumors alleged that Charlie and Gavin perpetrated an illegal infraction during the angling excursion. Erroneous events were the genesis of generosity.

Gavin vouched for Charlie. He convinced Danny and Mike to accept the qualified candidate as a clubmate. They willingly acceded. Charlie received an amended sobriquet and became a Ravalli County Rebel. The scamp's epithet was "Gnarly Charlie."

Four foraging fanatics explored streets and alleys until winter decreased depredation dramatically. Club members enlisted in the Cub Scouts of America during December. The rabble-rousing buddies were banished abruptly four months later.

All of the exiles had begrudged Cub Scouts governance guidelines. Danny, Gavin and Charlie also detested Mike's misguided mandates as the Ravalli County Rebels' leader. An insistent majority prevailed. The boys disbanded a broken bicycle brotherhood.

Three weeks after Cub Scouts of America excommunication the unrepentant upstarts met at their tree fort. They formulated an unprecedented subversive alliance. Gavin emulated a statesman while he explained, "We should have the same system Congress uses. When they make rules everything gets voted on. It's called parley mental procedure. An inept president can be ousted."

New club bylaws were finalized and the last contingency was deliberated. Mike preferred the designation Redneck Raiders but he conceded crabbily.

The chaos crusaders avowed a loyal oath. They swore fidelity to an outfit entitled the Bitterroot Brigade.

Mock warfare was vigorously validated as a healthy hobby for western Montana children. Massacre mimicry fostered fortitude and familiarized wide eyed whelps with weaponry. Squirts were swayed to simulate slaughter.

Parents purported pretend parricide perpetuated patriotism and prepared progeny properly. They acquired an array of toy rifles by the trainload. Plentiful plastic pistols and bazookas replicated real weapons remarkably. When wannabe soldiers aged their armaments appetite evolved. Army surplus gear was in high demand.

Poor weather postponed Bitterroot Brigade bicycle missions. The corps conducted boot camp in a swamp that surrounded their tree fort. One Saturday during early May it snowed six inches. The partisans wore white sheets like 10th Mountain Division infantrymen. They besieged scarecrows with slushball salvos. Other rehearsal skirmishes were undergone. The doughboys developed into an accomplished commando unit.

Summer vacation approached. The collaborators lacked feasible forays. Mike's aspiration to steal a cropduster's airplane and strafe dog doo doo droppings on their erstwhile Cub Scout den mother's abode was far-fetched. Gavin's gambit failed ratification. An inconspicuous release of a gazillion garden racer snakes in the girls bathroom seemed problematic.

Charlie's suggestion was an irreverent satire. He wanted to set the two story metal tube fire escape at Jefferson Elementary School ablaze with gasoline soaked combustibles and a bottle rocket barrage. The pyromaniac's prudent pals prevented pandemonium. His associates abhorred arson alternatives.

Danny sought to kidnap an entire Barbie doll collection and hold the figurines hostage until a chocolate chip cookie ransom was extorted. His sidekicks savored snack food but the pediophobia sufferers declined. Many other proposals were discussed and denied.

An inspiration manifested during a meeting at Charlie's residence. The club's conundrum was solved by Marvel Comics. Danny wielded an *Ant-Man* and expounded, "The answer is in this Honor House Products Company ad. We're too inexperienced to drive Sherman Tanks but we can operate a Polaris Nuclear Submarine."

Gavin and Charlie nodded agreeably. Mike opined an incompatible opinion. He had once severed a digit with an Amazing Finger Chopper Trick. The mishap prone protestor berated his buddies as he barked, "Comic book gadgets are hogwash. Invisible Ink is just overpriced lemon juice. We shouldn't order that junk."

Charlie mentioned a meritorious message in an *Outlaw Kid* as he argued, "I bought a Kung-Fu Karate

Manual and its accessories. The chapter '101 Ways to Incapacitate Gonads' is an indispensable resource. I still use the practice dummy and nerve center chart every day. My thumbs are lethal."

Gavin assessed the submersible promotion scrupulously. The perceptive pundit posited, "This is a genuine voyager because the seller charges seventy five cents for shipping. It's made of 200lb test material. We have $9.56 in the club fund."

Another debate fomented. Mike stayed averse to submarine scenarios and submitted an inadequate substitution. The contrarian crossly commented, "I would rather buy a bunch of decommissioned bayonets or gas masks." Danny held up the advertisement like an irrefutable Perry Mason evidence presentation. He pompously proffered, "The Polaris Sub is seven feet long. It features seats for two kids, steering controls, rockets, a periscope and an electric instrument panel."

The Bitterroot Brigade resolved to requisition a weapon of mass destruction. An additional logistic loomed. Discreet delivery was desired. Contentious conversation carried on until the club chose Cougar Manufacturing Incorporated as a clandestine cargo receiver. The establishment was owned by Gavin's father. He endorsed activities that didn't entail parental supervision. The 101st Airborne veteran reckoned combat games were wholesome. Butch believed boys should be busy.

Gavin secured shipment support diligently. The ambassador showed his self-employed elder an unblemished comic book promotion. He hesitantly inquired, "Me and the fellas want a Polaris Nuclear Submarine. We put $7.73 in an old coffee can for COD payment. Do you think the package could be sent to your office?" Butch recalled youthful follies fondly. The hijinks hierophant grinned and acquiesced, "Sure son."

A postal errand proceeded. Gavin mailed in the order form and updated his pals later that afternoon. The future shipmates enjoyed Drumstick ice cream treats behind Mr. Gelato's market while he divulged, "My dad's on board with our plan." Everyone was excited about the imminent nautical expedition. Even Mike favored maritime domination. The placated sourpuss speculated, "I'll sink an inflatable raft. Tourists are worse than mosquitos." It wouldn't be long until Honor House Prod. Inc. of Lynbrook, New York shipped a splendid Polaris Nuclear Submarine to the Bitterroot Brigade.

Reconnaissance occurred repeatedly. The squad scoured riverbanks for potential portage problems. They determined an appropriate submersible base sight. A goggles, swim fins and snorkels arsenal was amassed. The frogmen swam beneath Main Street's Bridge frequently. Locations were triangulated to torpedo adversaries accurately. The militia morphed into an amphibious team that would've made Navy Seals proud.

Five weeks passed and the parcel arrived. Butch delivered a 4ft x 4ft cardboard box to the family's garage. He then entered the house and spotted his wife as she cooked. The dutiful dad questioned, "Where's Gavin?" Mary topped an appetizing tuna casserole with potato chips. The mindful mother sighed while she replied, "That silly child ran upstairs ten minutes ago."

Butch knocked on his son's bedroom door and whispered, "Psst. Your submarine box is in our garage. When will you deploy it?" Gavin sprang up from a cluttered desk energetically. He blithely blabbed, "We decided to launch at the swimming hole early tomorrow morning if it came today. Can I visit the fellas before suppertime? They'll need the lowdown." Butch suppressed an impetuous snicker and smiled. The congenial father assented, "Go take care of business. May I tell my buddies about the unveiling?"

Gavin granted a grievous gaffe. He authorized his dad to reveal an abstruse Bitterroot Brigade pursuit. The rascal rashly responded, "Invite anyone you want."

Butch was amused by his scion's naive fervor. The bemused benefactor offered, "I'll bring root beer so you can christen your U-boat." Gavin hastily departed the domicile. Butch telephoned assorted acquaintances. The harbinger's peers had been comic book advertisement saps themselves. He could've sold tickets to the escapade that ensued.

After a restless Friday night the Bitterroot Brigade rendezvoused in an alley beside Gavin's house. They opened the garage's double doors and distinguished a baffling box. Mike scanned the cardboard crate while he criticized, "How's an actual submarine supposed to fit inside that tiny container?" Danny defended the commodity fervently. The appealer apprised, "Look at this label. It says assembly required."

The bickerers devised a U-boat mobilization strategy. They theorized bicyclists with an intact Polaris Nuclear Submarine possibly seemed suspicious. Another practicality prompted the plotters profoundly. The box would be easier to move than a seven foot submersible. An improvised riverside build was unanimously sanctioned.

A tool bucket and the cardboard carton were loaded within an adaptable homemade bike trailer that was hitched to Gavin's bicycle. The committed companions mounted four banana seat bikes. Their courageous convoy pedaled powerfully. They detoured the Main Street Bridge, descended a rough rutted path and reached an unoccupied shoreline. The perspiring pals parked. A muster of men perched on an embankment. Danny beheld the bystanders and blurted, "Why are so many people here?"

Gavin perceived he shouldn't have provided viewer participation permission. The bungler tried to conceal his blatant blunder. He flusteredly fibbed, "It's probably a birthday party."

Mike intuited treason. He glared and accused, "Fess up Gavin. Those dudes are your dad's cronies. Even Grandpa Joe's here. This mission was classified. Gavin's rat fink father spilled the beans big time. The submarine isn't built yet and there's an information leak."

Gavin fathomed further falsehoods were futile. The ruer contritely confessed, "My dad asked if he could tell a couple of chums and I told him it was okay." Mike continued to carp on Gavin's misstep. The scandalmonger growled, "Loose lipped tongue waggers sink submersibles. I bet that bully Stan Morris and his flunkies heard about the U-boat. They might ambush us with depth charges."

Butch's buddies cheered sonorously. Charlie recognized retreat would be cowardly. He waved at the watchers and exhorted, "It's too late to turn back now. Let's invade the beach!" Four gung ho wayfarers hoisted the box onto their shoulders. Spectator applause became an ovation.

Audience approval amplified as the junket juggernauts slogged through dry sand like pallbearers. The plodders halted and situated their freight on a small peninsula. Hillside hoopla quieted. The throng's muted anticipation was an eerie silence before a humiliation hurricane.

Charlie brandished his pocket knife, cut the box's tape and unfolded its lid. The intrepid boys evaluated eight fiberboards. Danny spoke for the stunned group when he yammered, "Where's our rassa-frassin'submarine?"

Confusion compounded and crowd chortles cascaded. Witnesses watched an inane farce flourish. Keystone Cop skits were nothing compared to the ludicrous extravaganza. Calamity created colossal comedy.

Four frustrated friends constructed the cardboard contrivance cantankerously. Their concoction discredited comic book promotional pictures. The counterfeit contraption approximated a rickety *Space Patrol* rocket ship. Another flagrant flaw was detected. The wretched watercraft had no keel section. It didn't take an astute Naval architect to deduce that bottomless U-boats won't float.

The phony vessel was less buoyant than a newspaper sloop. Danny lifted the hatch. It dislodged and disconnected directly. The incredulous imp inspected an abysmal helmsman's compartment as he squawked, "What happened to our instrument panel and periscope? I don't see missiles or torpedoes either. Check in the box. Maybe we missed something."

Mike grabbed a brochure and an order form from the shipping crate. He analyzed the pamphlets purposefully. The riled reader roared, "Fortify your U-boat! Get a $4.99 accessory kit today!" Mike ripped the leaflets and self righteously raged, "I warned you schmucks about sham submarine shakedowns!"

Charlie deflected an urge to harm Mike. The martial arts maven transferred tempestuousness and screamed, "Haachaa!" He executed a roundhouse kick that explosively removed the tail fins. Charlie knelt and corkscrew punched the hull with his fists like Bruce Lee. He heatedly hollered, "I'm an invincible Ninja!"

Gavin was also enraged by the situation. He bare knuckle bashed the bowsprit and venomously vowed, "I'll never order from Honor House again. They're crooks!" Mike joined the dismantle dynamically. The assailant stomped on pointless propeller parts and ranted, "Crush this crapola!" Danny vehemently hurled remnants skyward.

The foursome fulminated furiously. Rowdy rage resounded raucously. The demolishers destroyed a damnable disgrace. Cardboard segments were strewn haphazardly. The atrocity assaulters abated. They slumped dejectedly. The submarine slayers wept scornful tears and onlookers hurrahed heartily.

Gavin's father saw the stupendous spectacle's culmination. He whistled loudly and shouted, "Hush your heckles." The gawkers guffaws ceased. Butch retrieved four bottles of root beer. He trotted to the worn out whippersnappers and sympathetically consoled, "Bad luck fellas. Who wants soda pops?"

The bamboozled boys swigged their soft drinks and Gavin bitterly bellyached, "That flippin' fake was useless." Butch scratched his chin while he rationally recommended, "Your U-boat trash would be good for a bonfire. We're gonna roast elk sausages and potatoes."

Four demoralized decimators transported Polaris Nuclear Submarine scraps to an enormous fire pit. Cardboard and wood were stacked inside the rock ring. Gavin's Grandpa Joe walked up with a Zippo. He ignited the pyre and counseled, "You rapscallions should always remember sometimes geniuses start life as fools."

Decades elapsed expeditiously. Gavin was fifty-nine years old. He resolutely bypassed impulse purchases. The smart shopper scrutinized sales spiels sagely. If an item or service seemed implausible Gavin wouldn't spend. The smug senior citizen comprehended he couldn't be conned.

A spurious scheme quashed Gavin's ego. He vetted an innovative garden shed after meticulous internet research. The superb structure had a five star rating. An enthusiastic review related, "I'm so happy. Setup is simple and it looks fantastic." Gavin ordered the sheet metal storage hut.

Two massive boxes arrived six weeks later. Gavin and his spouse began to erect the shed kit on a recently poured concrete pad in their backyard. An arduous debacle germinated. Gavin grouched gratingly. Mrs. Reynolds abandoned the protracted project permanently.

A plethora of preposterous production processes were performed partnerless posthaste.

The shed's paper manual was patently printed for an illiterate. Thirty pages of rudimentary drawings contained a one sentence annotation. The document's only written words stated, "Online advice at www.youstupidyankee.com." Gavin booted up his desktop. The website inflicted an abominable wormhole virus and a cherished Compaq computer crashed.

Gavin reverted to the hardcopy handout. Senseless sequences skipped steps. Dozens of dreadful diagrams were undecipherable. Gavin had built with wood but the metal monstrosity was an enigma. The undaunted do it yourself tinsmith forged ahead fastidiously.

A spate of impalement injuries preceded the eighty square foot challenge's complex completion. Gavin stood defiantly beside his finished piece de resistance and declared, "I stymied those sneaky shysters." The guy with twenty gash wounds obsession subsided. He relished a peaceful moment.

Gavin awoke early the next morning after overnight rain. The consummate craftsman went outside. He slid the shed's door sideways smoothly and instantly espied an extraordinary attribute of his latest triumph. Obviously the fabulous fabrication functioned as a wading pool.

The roof didn't leak but liquid filled an inundated floor. Gavin's maddened mutters multiplied monumentally. He hee-hawed hysterically. His chuckles caterwauled clamorously. It was a noise that often accompanies an anxiety attack.

Gavin unleashed a curse word cannonade. His prolific philosophical pronouncements were profane. The resentful ranter raved, "Sons of matriarchal mongrels. This shed is fan freaking fracking frucking tastic. Imported puppy poop will put me in an imbecilic flunking funny farm someday!"

The outraged outbuilding owner stared at his watery reflection. He morosely mused, "The devil's in details dunkoff." Gavin sloshed to a workbench, picked up an immense magnifying glass and studied a microscopic sticker on the window frame.

An almost imperceptible address appeared. Honor House Products Company had relocated headquarters from Lynbrook, New York to Shanghai, China. The corrupt corporation's conspiracy converted. Few children read comic books in the digital age. Copious cyber codgers coveted cheap sheds.

Gavin suddenly discerned a lifelong gullibility liability. Despite diverse duplicitous disappointments the trustful tyke mindset remained an internal companion. Although Gavin's piquant personality conveyed a crotchety curmudgeon veneer he was an unreformed optimist. The hermit habitually hoped for honest humanity. He once said, "Kindness can be costly but it's worth every cent of consideration. Principled paupers

live in light and malevolent misers dwell amidst
darkness."

The Bitterroot Brigade

Geese filled the Montana sky and frost crystallized Ravalli County countryside. The timeline for Operation Gauntlet was short. Educational institutionalization impeded Gavin, Mike, Danny and Charlie's efforts. The cohorts occupied Jefferson Elementary School desks. They watched a clock amidst an October afternoon while their whiskey inebriated teacher snored.

A bell woke Mr. Stephens. He smacked his lips and slurred, "Class dismissed." The scamps sped out of an ajar door. They sprinted down a stairwell and burst through the exit as an office secretary shrieked, "Slow down! Our halls aren't a racetrack!" The misbehavers mounted their bicycles. Each rider accelerated away at an impressive velocity.

Mike picked up a bundle of newspapers from the Ravalli Republic office and met his three buddies at an indiscreet location behind Mr. Gelato's market. The aged Italian immigrant contributed to a conspiracy which subverted Hamilton's information source. He openly opined, "Their ad rates are an insult."

A clandestine arrangement was necessary because of middle management meddlers. Regulations required one delivery person. The boys slurped root beer and rubber banded rolled newspapers skillfully. Their revenue routine subsidized emboldened endeavors.

The allies against authority burdened backpacks with bulletins. Danny, Gavin, Charlie and Mike set off separately to distribute an individual portion of the route efficiently. Their tactic facilitated additional unsupervised pursuits.

Newspaper deliveries were consummated and the pals pedaled onwards determinedly. They swarmed into the swamp that surrounded their tree fort. The purposeful cyclists parked and climbed a nearby rope ladder. Another advantageous defiance of decrees was done.

The friends functioned as an ambitious enterprise. A democratic document dictated decorum. Their club charter was entitled, "The Bitterroot Brigade Declaration of Independence, Constitution and Bylaws."

According to the meritorious manifesto leadership rotated monthly. Mike served as commander when the committed colleagues plotted their latest expedition. He earnestly expounded, "We must press forward with our classified mission code named Operation Gauntlet. An appropriations agenda needs approval."

Four hotheads heatedly haggled until Danny wrote a requisition list. An accepted compendium comprised:

4-Inner Tubes*
2-Rubber Repair Kits*
?-Potato Chips, Ding Dongs, Root Beer & Candy*
4-Rucksacks
4-Bicycle Tire Pumps

2-Standard Pocket Knives
1-Swiss Army Knife
1-Box Cutter
2-Snorkels
1-Scuba Mask
3-Flashlights
2-Walkie Talkies
6-Seven Foot Rodeo Rope Lengths

The Bitterroot Brigade comprehended they lacked starred checklist items. Mike addressed the logistical snags. He banged an oxidized meat tenderizer gavel and sanctioned, "We'll confiscate components. Alley trash cans, garages, attics, basements, pantries and sibling's bedrooms are to be ransacked. Club conference concluded."

A stellar stockpile amassed but the accomplices still sought six essential pieces of equipment. Two days remained before Operation Gauntlet. An emergency conclave was assembled at the tree fort. Mike controlled conversation as he coerced, "The logical place to obtain inner tubes and rubber repair kits is Red's Gas Station."

Gavin was averse because of his grandfather's employment at the establishment. He adamantly protested, "You're despicable. Grandpa Joe's a saint." Mike interrupted the objection intentionally. The instigator insisted, "I motion we purchase inner tubes and rubber repair kits from Red's Gas Station." Charlie suddenly seconded. An immediate three to one vote followed.

Mike promptly predicated, "Next order of business." Charlie spoke swiftly. The abettor advanced, "I motion we create a cover story. An alibi will be handy."

Gavin sensed something was amiss and his suspicions swelled after Mike submitted a supportive statement. The contriver contended, "Grandpa Joe shouldn't hear about Operation Gauntlet. We'll tell him an itsy bitsy white lie. I second Charlie."

Three vocal voters favored fictionalization forthwith. Gavin perceived his pals precisely planned parlance. The doubter's distrust developed as Danny divulged, "I motion Gavin buys inner tubes and rubber repair kits. I also motion he tells Grandpa Joe it's for a school project."

Charlie commented on cue. The colluder conferred, "I second both of Danny's motions." An abrupt verdict was merciless. Three yahoos yodeled yeas and Gavin yawped nay.

Mike pounded the culinary hammer as he exhorted, "Meeting adjourned!" The sophist soon soothed Gavin's sore sentiments. Mike sensibly solaced, "Our fib protects Grandpa Joe. It's called plausible delinquency."

The preoccupied pundits ascertained suppertime. They evacuated the tree fort and hastened homeward like demented rickshaw drivers. Upset mothers awaited them. Unpunctuality potentially precipitated penalties. Luckily the transgressor's tardiness was treated as a tolerable trespass because an electrical outage delayed dinner.

When the weary boys laid in their beds later that evening they heard Montana melodies. A lumber laden train clickety clacked from Darby to Missoula. An elk's whistle echoed resonantly. The Bitterroot River's low autumn waters murmured a lullaby. Its soporific serenade summoned serene sleep.

Pretense was polished before the prevaricators procured inner tubes and rubber repair kits. They rehearsed roles during Thursday's lunch recess. Mike impersonated Grandpa Joe. Charlie acted as teenage gas pump jockey Pete. Danny portrayed an entire ensemble of extras. Gavin played Gavin.

Practice progressed and Gavin discerned a single falsehood in the dialog was his alone. The displeased deceiver warned, "None of us will take anything without Grandpa Joe's permission."

Classes ceased at 3pm. The Bitterroot Brigade rallied and rode to Red's Gas Station. They parked behind an International Harvester tow truck surreptitiously. The scoundrels then bought root beers from a soda machine and entered an office noiselessly. Various car seats circled a wooden checkerboard. The gametable was where old men argued politics and told tall tales. Their aggrandized anecdotes were as Danny described, "Visions of grand turds."

An ecru Dodge Dart bench seat was vacant so the voiceless visitors sat down. They listened to the pensioner's whoppers politely. The devious boys rationed their beverages. Minutes ticked on a Valvoline clock that hung beside an outdated Pennzoil pinup calendar.

Grandpa Joe finally asked, "How are you fellas today?" Mike respectfully replied, "We're fantastic sir." The hoodwinker smiled surely. He slouched and subtly elbowed Gavin. The moment of untruth arrived.

Gavin glimpsed at the floor as he muttered, "May we buy four inner tubes and a couple of rubber repair kits?" Grandpa Joe's expression was unreadable. The stoic cleared his throat and questioned, "What do you rascals want car stuff for?"

Boisterous banter paused. The spectators became silent and still. An uneasy mein materialized. Suspense ended after Gavin paltered, "It's for a school science experiment." Grandpa Joe nodded and chuckled until he offered, "Just as I thought you're four scholars. Let's scrounge some supplies."

Gavin's generous grandfather donated inner tubes and rubber repair kits. The perjurers placed particulars in backpacks while they thanked Grandpa Joe. Danny, Charlie, Mike and Gavin walked to their bikes. An uproar of laughter resounded from Red's Gas Station as the deluders rode away.

The swag smugglers eluded intervention. They stashed the inner tubes and repair kits at their tree fort. The complicit pals proceeded home. Gavin's dishonesty fostered nighttime regret. He stared out the bedroom window somberly. The melancholy youngster fell asleep and drowsed in a discomfited dreamworld.

An extensive sortie schedule was reviewed repeatedly during a Friday forum. The tenacious team packed rucksacks competently. Every contingency had been considered. Preparations finalized and Mike related, "We meet up here first thing tomorrow morning."

Two weeks before the quest commenced Gavin discovered an aqueduct entrance when he skipped a piano lesson at Mrs. Harrison's house. An inconspicuous irrigation canal tunnel threshold was situated near the music tutor's lawn. Gavin subsequently revealed the culvert to his clubmates. A befuddled Bitterroot Brigade watched as water disappeared into darkness and Danny stammered, "An inner tube ride through that passage would be a gutsy gauntlet."

Deployment day dawned. The boys mustered at their tree fort and retrieved backpacks They then pedaled towards an uncertain fate. A jaunt to an empty lot between the Safeway Store and Burlington Northern's railroad tracks avoided interception. The confident crew parked. Each provocateur abandoned his bike and ambled along a prearranged approach route. An orchestrated nonchalance thwarted tattletales.

The resolved raiders reached Mrs. Harrison's residence. A scan of the scene showed no snoops. Hand signal communication was conducted covertly. The stealthy troop loped to an apt ditch access point. Shrubbery cloaked the site perfectly. The commandos unpacked paraphernalia. Inner tubes were inflated and roped together.

Danny donned his official Jacques Cousteau diving mask. Bicycle pumps were stowed in rucksacks. The rogues shouldered their carryalls, grabbed flashlights and radios. The synchronized squad jettisoned their crude craft into shallow water. Each diver lept on the raft dexterously. The proficient platoon proved prior preparation prevents poor performance.

Four adept aquanauts drifted downstream. Mike wielded a walkie talkie and tested an initial transmission. The buoyant broadcaster barked, "Radio check. Roger Alpha One!" Charlie clicked the correspondent communicator confusedly. The wireless gadget was mute. Mike attempted to send another message when he hastily hollered, "Radio check. Roger Beta Two."

The rubber raft wranglers recognized there was a technical malfunction. Mike brusquely bayed, "Dagnabit is the other unit turned on?" Charlie flusteredly fingered the temperamental transceiver. After an instant he woefully wailed, "The son of a gun's stupid switch seized."

Mike demonstrated steely nerves. He adapted and overcame. The steadfast stalwart shouted, "Forget our gosh dang radios. Full steam ahead!"

The perilous portal was proximate. Danny nervously inquired, "Do you guys think this is smart? Maybe we should turn back." Apprehension also affected Gavin and Charlie's demeanor. Mike detected mutiny. The livid leader loudly lambasted, "Buck up! The Bitterroot Brigade ain't no place for wafflers!"

Mike's mandate prevented desertion. The wary swabbies infiltrated an enigmatic subterranean canal corridor. They were ten feet inside the tunnel when a terrible torment transpired. An icky stringy substance entangled each horrified kid's head. The frenzied friends frantically fulminated. A cattywampus kerfuffle continued until Mike urged, "All flashlights on."

The rattled rafters heard an ominous kerplunk before Danny kvetched, "Shoot I dropped my expensive Sears Explorer." Charlie's damp D cell device flickered and went out. Gavin triggered the last electric torch. Its dim beam illuminated a ghastly sight and fear fomented.

Scared shrill screams sounded severely. The cavern was choked with gazillions of gossamer growths. Each enmeshed encroacher exclaimed, "Spiders!" The panic stricken pals plunged sideways. No craniums conked the cement ceiling coincidentally. The terrified tetrad surfaced and clutched raft corners. Arachnid encounters were averted but Gavin's Penguin penlight vanished. An eerie umbra ensued.

The startled quartet stayed mostly submersed and swam. No one squawked a syllable for several seconds. Only splashes were audible. An acute claustrophobia crisis was confirmed when Charlie cawed, "This creek is cruddy!" Danny fumed futilely. The dismayed decrier declared, "What a diabolical debacle!" Gavin discarded civility. The bellyacher blurted, "Holy shrimp!" Mike perpetuated perseverance. He resiliently roared, "Keep your skulls safe and hang on!"

An unlit chasm compelled consternation. The perplexed partisans psyches pondered personal perishability. A vague glow in the distance eventually emanated. The swimmers' tacit trepidation amplified to an invigorated chorus of cheers. They beheld a tunnel terminus. Danny espied the egress and exuberantly extolled, "Excellent!" His elation was accompanied as Charlie dramatically declared, "We made it!"

Gavin verified the valiant voyager's victory. He wildly whooped, "Hot diggity dog!" Former foray fiascos faded when Mike proclaimed an impromptu proud pronouncement. The relieved ringleader rejoiced, "Land ho!"

Daylight deluged the drenched drifters. They waded to the shore and dismantled their raft. The contented canal conquerors resembled methodical muskrats. Inner tubes were deftly deflated. The saturated stream subduers loaded gear into soaked backpacks and reclaimed bicycles. A drippy dash finished at the tree fort.

An audacious extravaganza actualized. The ecstatic chums gorged themselves on Hostess Ding Dongs, Lay's potato chips and Red Vines licorice. Charlie inhaled a Kings candy cigarette before he cackled, "Congratulations comrades!"

Gavin uncapped four root beer bottles and handed three of the refreshments to his confidants. The spirited server held an effervescent elixir aloft as he triumphantly toasted, "Bitterroot Brigade bravery. Hurrah!" Danny, Mike and Charlie supplemented Gavin's salutation. The pals professed a profound credo when they vehemently vowed, "Carpe Libertas!"

The gallant guild savored success until an aberration appeared. Danny saw a pustule on Charlie's forehead and inferred, "The nutcase must've hit his noggin. Look at that lump." The ridiculer pointed towards an ambiguous brow bump. Danny's limb was blemished with a bunch of burgundy bulges. Gavin, Mike and Charlie caterwauled, "Hives!"

An unprecedented party terminated tumultuously. The disastrous dermatology demise destroyed delirium. Rapture was replaced by misery and despair. Bevies of boils broke out on each boy. The casualties clawed cankerous clumps like flea infested hounds as they tried to tame their inflammations. Insatiable itchiness exceeded poison ivy and nettles.

Mike decided decisiveness was deemed. He hurriedly hooted, "Let's smear ourselves with mud." The kibitzer's recommendation received glares as Gavin groaned, "Golly Geronimo! My precious jewels are on fire!" The swollen scrotum sufferer's companions conjointly complained. Charlie soon lamented, "We're doomed" and Danny predicted, "Our moms will murder us."

The three defeatists rankled Mike. He accosted his associate's attitudes and asininely admonished, "Why don't you wusses shut your pieholes!" Mike's monocratic mind misjudged. Charlie brandished both fists and yowled, "Do you want a knuckle sandwich?"

Danny also resented Mike's reprimand. He snarkily snarled, "You can stick salami where the sun don't shine!" Charlie and Danny started to shove Mike. The tempestuous trio tussled until Gavin thundered, "Stop!"

Harmony became anarchy. An accursed maniacal madness inflicted the arguers. Epidermal eruptions elevated and empathy evaporated. The cantankerous chaffers confronted comprehensive cognitive collapse.

Gavin surmised a possible solution. The purple skinned problem solver proffered, "Grandpa Joe has medic training. Perhaps he'll help us. I motion we talk to my granddad."

Mike spouted support succinctly. The corroborator concurred, "I second that motion." Gavin's proposal was rapidly ratified even though Charlie refused participation. The furious fiend frowned forcefully and rabidly twitched. His hostile histrionics halted as he howled, "This sucks King Kong monkey trucker butts!" Mike, Gavin and Danny agreed in unison before they descended the rope ladder.

Rampant roseola spread like an intense inferno. Profuse paresthesia pimples pulsated. The scallywags straddled bikes scrupulously. Puffy private parts forced the blistered bicyclists to stand while they rode towards Red's Gas Station. The rash recipients reached their destination despite difficulties.

Grandpa Joe labored beneath a Plymouth Duster's hood when the troubled tykes limped through an open back door. The master mechanic witnessed woeful waifs as they writhed. Each fidgeter's festered face displayed dozens of noticeable nodes. The slant six engine specialist couldn't contain amusement. Grandpa Joe chortled convulsively and crowed, "You boys are a bedraggled bunch. What happened?"

Gavin disclosed Operation Gauntlet details thoroughly. Grandpa Joe scowled and shook his head. The deception disappointed him deeply.

Grandpa Joe rasped as he reproached the ragamuffins resolutely. The aggravated grandfather glared and growled, "So you simpletons floated with the inner tubes I provided. Do you dimwits have any idea how many children drown in ditches?"

All of the ruer's eyes streamed tears. Grandpa Joe let his grievance's gravity grow briefly. He then imparted mercy. The charitable senior citizen stipulated, "I'll assist you dunces on two conditions. You dingbats must never lie to me or swim in irrigation canals again."

The pockmarked pack pledged, "Yes Sir." Grandpa Joe reflected temporarily and instructed, "Here's what you dummies are gonna to do. When your mothers pester about the allergy you imbeciles will say my pond's murky water is toxic."

Grandpa Joe produced five dollar bills from his pocket and prescribed, "Go to Bitterroot Drug. Buy four bottles of calamine lotion. If you morons return home with medicine maybe your folks won't fuss too much." Gavin lunged and hugged the philanthropic patriarch tightly. The remorseful juvenile whispered, "I'm sorry. I love you Grandpa Joe."

An elderly man sat at his kitchen counter and sipped coffee. Gavin recollected boyhood. He persistently penciled another outlandish narrative outline in a notebook. Montana misadventure memories manifested marginally mythical manuscripts. The farcical fablist frequently said, "Although alliteration abides as an antiquated art absurdity activates altruism. Grammatical gags germinate guffaws and goodness."

www.ingramcontent.com/pod-product-compliance
Lightning Source LLC
Chambersburg PA
CBHW030343180626
46812CB00007B/2742